Published by Dragon Brothers Books Ltd
www.dragonbrothersbooks.com
Text © 2021 James Russell.
ISBN: 978-0-473-55935-9
Cover image: Soar Earth
Cover design: Trevor Finnegan, revertdesign.net
Book design: Suzanne Denmead

SALTWATER SERIES

MINE

James Russell

*"A ship is safe in harbour,
but that's not what ships are for."*

J.A. Shedd

Chapter 1

The day the Brazilian boys were murdered, the surf was so good it's impossible to do it justice in writing. I remember it with a hard-edged clarity, a laser focus; I'd sat for a while on the beach, wholly hypnotised. If I close my eyes now I can feel the warm trade wind at my back, the coarse sand scrunching in my hands.

That day, sets arrived from the open sea in endless, ordered, regimental ranks. As they sensed the reef, the swells rose still higher, forming great, glossy walls in such abundance it was like some sort of oceanic production line. Each wave, darkened by the sheer volume of water it contained, suddenly glowed like a jewel as it thinned and reared and toppled, backlit by the rising sun.

Wave after sublime wave furled across the reef; spinning glass cylinders, huffing clouds of misting spit from their bellies out into the morning air.

On the other side of the reef pass, the right was almost the perfect mirror image.

I was happy to just watch it for a while, knowing that it would break like this all day, right through the tides. No one was coming to ruin it. No one would ever come.

I remember speaking out loud.

"Mine," I said.

Mine.

The Sentinelese kids sat all around, as glued to me as I was to the waves. I'd become so used to them following me I hardly noticed them any more.

Taking in the mesmerising vision before me, I recall that I raised my arms towards the ocean like an idiot king acknowledging his subjects. My own surfing realm. Every single wave that broke on this reef was mine. It felt wasteful, extravagant, almost obscene. I can't deny that I had an impulse to share it, to tell someone else about what I had. It was the same impulse felt by every other surfer who'd ever discovered a new break.

I spoke out loud again, I remember, a babble of self-reproach. I called myself stupid, and crazy, and a fucking idiot. The kids all looked at me, but they were used to it by then.

It broke the spell. I remember picking up my board and trying to ignore the fact that the nose of it was gone, shortened by six inches the week prior from a collision with the reef. I'd been horrified, stricken with dread. I'd dried it in the sun, then packed it with fish oil and grass, but I knew it was hopeless. The foam was browning, the stain travelling down the board, disappearing under my chest.

I decided on the left. The set that swept through the bay just before I paddled out is etched in my mind. The biggest of the morning, the first wave crumbled and avalanched, sending a white tongue of foam sliding down its face. It seemed like some sort of personal courtesy to my surfing ability that the bigger it got out here, the easier the takeoff became. Then, as the wave felt the pull of the reef, it stood, launching its muscular lip shoreward.

It chandeliered, slabs of water falling one after another like chunks of ice breaking from a glacier. It looked as though it might close out, but I knew that it wouldn't. It never did.

Sixty metres down the line and the wave slowed to a grind, a vertical face chased by a foaming spume ball, like looking into the belly of a concrete truck.

Then, once again, the wave picked up pace; a uniform acceleration. The speed run. It hollowed itself out, moving with mechanical precision, a cylinder on a factory lathe. It spun like this for another hundred metres across the shallowest part of the reef.

In a last act, a prolonged exhalation of spray burst from the closing mouth of the barrel, the cloud of vapour dissipating like a magic trick.

When the Brazilians arrived I'd had about a dozen of those waves. I hadn't fallen once. The roll-ins took my breath away. There was time to stand upright, to marvel at the pure power pulsing beneath my feet. It was like big HTs, but reversed, and without all the fuckwits in the way. A lazy, drawn-out drop, my board thrumming with speed, a little fade and an easy bottom turn. All that was required was the subtlest of checks as the floor dropped out and the lip threw. That first barrel was the easiest. I rode it deeper every time, the chandeliers falling from the roof like the cogs of some huge machine. Then, as the tube spat and the wave slowed, I fizzed out onto the face and stood tall for a moment, arching my back, a smile pasted across my stupid, sunburned face. I tried to do those cutties that Parko does – travelling a mile out on the face, rising, rising, and then downcarving in a speeding arc until I could line up a bounce off the whitewater.

Through the middle of each wave I tried to hook ever harder in the pocket, sometimes free-falling back down the face. One, two, three, four turns, and then it was all about setting up for the grand finale; the hundred-metre sprint to the finish line.

It's shockingly shallow, that part of the reef, and where I often came unstuck, but not that day. A continuous, transparent sheet-glass guillotine sliced its way along the crystalline conveyor, gathering ever more speed until it breathed like a dragon into the channel. I got so far back in those barrels that I could feel the foam ball snapping at my heels.

And then the Brazos showed up. I saw their boat from a long way off, but seeing boats in the distance was nothing unusual. Then they turned in my direction.

Until I could make them out properly I thought it might be just some plucky local fisherman coming to try out his luck in the danger zone. But as they got closer I made out a familiar shape poking up in the bow of the boat – a board bag. I remember the electrical pulse that went through me, through my gut, up my spine; it comes back to me now just thinking of it. There were two of them, dark heads bobbing as they rose and fell over the swells. Their boat was the same as all the Andaman fishing boats – a long wooden skiff, brightly painted.

Soon I was in no doubt – they were coming. As I watched, one of them pointed in my direction; they'd seen me.

I remember raising my arms above my head, palms towards them. Frantically, I jerked my hands, as though I could push them away. But on they came, faster now, planing through the pass.

I sat on my board then, dumbfounded. A fog, a paralysis, filled my head. I got caught inside up by a wave that I hadn't even noticed coming, and when I surfaced the two lads were hooting like crazy and dropping the anchor. They ripped their boards from the covers and threw them over the side, diving in after them.

It was then that I took my first glance back at the shore. I saw the kids run along the beach and disappear into the forest. My chest felt tight and it was like all the energy had been sucked from my arms. I paddled as hard as I could towards the visitors, but I was well inside and they'd almost reached the take-off spot by the time I made it out the back again. An eight-foot bomb reeled along the reef like a freight train.

"Faaarrrk!" screamed one of the boys, and he paddled even harder, frothing to get amongst it. His mate followed on his heels. They were both about my age – somewhere in their twenties – and tattooed and tanned and fit. They weren't the least bit afraid of the huge surf surging through the lineup.

I remember the relief I felt as I paddled over that wave and saw that there was a lull. There was still time.

"Brah!" one of them yelled to me. He started babbling excitedly in Portuguese but I cut him off.

"Fuck off!" I yelled. I was gasping for breath.

The Brazo smiled at his mate and then turned back to me. "Come on, man," he said. "You have to share with your new friends. What the fuck – are you naked?"

"You have to go," I yelled. "You don't understand. They'll kill you."

"Ah, OK, brah, no problem. We'll go." Grinning, he lay down on his board and took a few strokes towards their boat. Then he stopped, laughed, and sat back up on his board.

"Get fucked," said his mate, smiling. He was looking out to sea, rising up on his board, and I knew the next set was coming.

"You'll die if you stay here!" I yelled.

"So they'll kill us, but they let you surf here all by yourself? Nice try, man."

"Listen to me," I pleaded. "This is North Sentinel Island. They will fucking kill you. They're coming already. You have to leave."

The Brazo looked towards the shore. "I don't see anyone."

"They're coming!" I yelled.

But the set had arrived, and the boys had picked their waves. They paddled side by side, lying low and flat against their boards, kicking for speed.

I followed them, but I knew there was nothing I could do. They wanted just one thing; to surf these waves. I knew exactly how they felt.

They caught the first two waves of that set, confidently getting to their feet, their eyes already scanning down the line. Both were better surfers than I was, and part of me thrilled to see these waves being so expertly ridden. They threaded those first tubes with a nonchalant ease, and as they continued down the reef I saw great rooster tails of spray sent skyward through the mid-section of the wave.

I looked back at the beach, trying to see what was happening through the atomised vapour of the pounding surf. Six men were already dragging two dugouts down the beach. They leapt in and set to paddling, the thin hulls slicing through the water. By the time the Brazos kicked out into the channel, the dugouts were well clear of the beach. I saw the two boys look back towards them, but I could see from the way they moved that they weren't alarmed. The Sentinelese didn't appear to be carrying weapons, but I knew they'd have them in the bottom of the canoes.

A medium-sized wave approached and I stroked hard for it, almost missing it, and only just getting to my feet as it pitched. I just made the drop and got out onto the face, and then pumped down the line.

I pulled off when I reached the boys. They were charged, jabbering to each other, paddling hard to get out for another one, but when I yelled to them and pointed at the canoes racing towards us they finally seemed to understand.

"Are you fucking serious, man?" said one of them, and I screamed at them to go and they changed direction, now paddling for their boat. Fear distorted their faces.

I paddled directly out, across the pass, trying to get into the path of the leading canoe. As it got closer I saw one of them set down his paddle and make his way to the bow. My hope dissolved when I realised it was Joro. He shouted to the paddlers and the canoe veered away, arcing around me, so I paddled again to get in its road.

Joro stood up on the bow and bared his teeth at me, hissing like a viper. He drew back an arrow and aimed at me and I simply stopped paddling, frozen with terror.

"Suna, Joro! No!" I screamed, but they were gone past me, and I couldn't paddle fast enough to catch them.

The Brazos were halfway to their boat, but Joro bore down on them, and I saw him shout a command for the paddlers to halt. One of the Brazo boys had stopped and sat up on his board and he turned to face Joro, his hands in the air, pleading for his life. He was crying and shaking like a leaf.

I screamed at Joro once more, but he didn't even turn around. I saw him take careful aim, cold and unhurried, and loose the arrow.

Chapter 2

SIX MONTHS EARLIER

It's a cruel irony that I'm at the peak of my surfing ability and I hate it more than ever. Today's going to be no different. It's not even 6am and there isn't a carpark to be found on Snapper Rocks Road. There are fuckwits everywhere, pulling on their wetties and smearing zinc across their faces. They're waxing up retro twin fins and fishes even though it's still too dark to see what the surf's doing.

I'm repelled, as usual, by the whole circus. It makes me feel like a junkie as I cruise the streets looking for a parking spot – as much as I hate what surfing has become I always seem to need to go back for more.

I'm at the far end of Greenmount before I see a space and I speed down the street to beat a shitty Corolla with six boards on the roof. How the hell do you get all your mates together at this time of the morning?

I get out of the car. There's not a breath of wind, and the sound from the ocean is encouraging – a steady roar, without the crack and rumble of discernible waves. Might be bigger than they were giving.

I suit up and wax my board – a 6'4" Hammo I bought last week. This'll be its christening. I lock the car and stick the keys in the suspension cup. Despite myself, I've got a bit of a froth on.

I'm halfway to Snapper when I realise I've forgotten my earplugs. The doctor said they'd have to operate if the bone growth gets any worse; she couldn't even see past it to my eardrums. I run back to the car and the keys drop out of the suspension cup and fall behind the wheel and I have to lie on the ground and feel around behind the tyre to get them. I'm already sweating.

By the time I re-stash the keys and jog back to Snapper there's just enough light to see that it's going to be a classic day. Lines are pouring around the corner, and I can make out the fingers of white water steadily extending themselves across the bay. It's hard to tell, but it looks solid; maybe six foot. It was blowing offshore last night, but now there's not a puff, so it's going to be glassy.

At the keyhole there are so many people that I have to wait my turn to get in the water. When I peer out into the gloom, my heart sinks; there's enough light to see that there are already fifty or sixty people bobbing in the lineup. They're strung out all the way down to Greenmount, like bluebottles on fly paper.

As I paddle out, I hold onto a slim hope that there might not be as many behind the rock, but the further I get I can see that it's a fucking zoo there too. I almost turn around right there and then, but I'm almost out so figure I may as well try to snag one or two.

It's heartbreakingly good: a surfer rips past me at warp speed, threading a fizzing toboggan track. A facsimile – its carbon copy – follows, then another, each sending its rider hurtling down the line. It's spellbinding, seductive.

I decide fuck it, I'll head to the top of the point, and I take my place at the edge of a twenty-man scrum behind the rock. They're so close together you could throw a tarp over them.

The local crew are holding court, yakking and screeching at each other. They're like seagulls fighting over fallen chips. I met a Kiwi bloke once who cheekily told me that Kiwis and Aussies sound just like the native birds of their respective countries. Birds in New Zealand all sound like they're playing the flute, he said, while Aussie birds sound as if they've swallowed angle grinders. Listening to this lot, he wasn't wrong.

I spot Mick Fanning, sitting in pole position as usual. A bomb looms and he lazily paddles for it, getting to his feet in that liquid way that he does. For a second I think he's fucked it up because he's high up on the face, but he just air-drops into it and parks himself inside the yawning barrel with nonchalant ease. He's lost from view as the wave passes by, but I see a jet a water sent skyward thirty metres down the line. He'll be gone for five minutes on a day like this.

There are more waves in the set, and the locals disappear one by one. I paddle up hard to the back of the pack, and a couple of them shoot me a look. They know me, but they pretend not to. Another set passes and more of them are gone, but Mick's back and he paddles straight to the inside. He doesn't even grin as he takes the next wave; he just expects it. No one says shit to him.

Fifteen minutes pass and I reckon I'm the only one in the pack that hasn't caught a wave, so it's time to man up. I paddle inside everyone, and ignore the scowls. The fuckers know full well it's my turn. Mick's back again, but he seems satiated, and is chatting to a mate at the back of the pack.

As we wait two of them paddle inside me again, so I paddle inside them. No one says a word. I'm way too deep now, but there's nothing I can do about it without relinquishing my position.

I hate this shitty chess game at Snapper. There's no honour, no honesty. The hostility in the lineup is palpable, with everyone throwing daggers at each other. And when a wave shows up, we're like dingoes tearing at a carcass.

My wave has arrived. Its beautiful broad back swells, a long, tapering wall forming as it rises out of the bay. I paddle for the shoulder, knowing that some greasy fuckwit has paddled inside me, but I ignore him, and he knows I'm not going to pull back. I don't even look at him as I turn for the wave. Smearing myself against my board, I stroke hard into it. In the corner of my eye I see him paddling too, but as I begin to slide he pulls back.

It's never an easy take off behind the rock, but this isn't the sand-sucking Frankenstein some of them can be. Still, it's a chunky wave and my heart's in my mouth as I make the drop and lean into a bottom turn for all I'm worth. My front foot's hard on the rail, and there's no skitter; The Hammo feels like a marvel under my feet.

The surface is like blown glass. I knife hard, but still only just make it, sneaking under the cascading curtain by a whisker. The crack of the lip as it detonates on the surface is like a rifle shot, and I'm suddenly the bullet in the barrel. There's a savage acceleration and I struggle to hold my line, pigdogging like crazy, but then it seems to set of its own accord and I'm locked in. Time appears to slow. I'm suddenly aware of everything – my fingers trailing in the wall, the spinning vortex all around me. I flex and adjust without thinking. I'm anticipating what's going to happen, and I get one of those glimpses you sometimes get of what it must be like to be a better surfer than you are. The wave is gorgeously uniform – there's no closeout section in sight. The sun has risen and the wall is a shimmering, liquid sapphire.

The moment I come to the realisation that this will be one of the waves of my life, I see the guy down the line turn and paddle. For my wave. He's framed by the falling lip. He doesn't even look back at me. He simply puts his head down and goes. I watch as he's pulled back up the face, trying in vain to get to his feet. He's sucked up the face, the section beneath him collapses, and the last thing I see before I'm swallowed up is him going over the falls.

We surface in a maelstrom of foam and tangled boards. I'm ropeable.

"What the fuck?" I scream at him, but before the next wave comes we have to get our leg ropes apart, which have intertwined and now our boards are bashing together. We don't make it in time and the next wave is upon us, a surfer locked into its churning barrel. But someone else drops in on him, and I dive deep to avoid them both. When I come up my board is somehow freed, and the first fuckwit has washed further in. I catch the next wave in on my guts and shout a 'fuck you' to him as I pass. He replies in like fashion.

Walking up the beach, I see the ragged gash in the underside of my brand new Hammo. It's about the same size as the middle finger that I turn and present to Snapper Rocks.

Chapter 3

My name is James Brennan and I'm 26 years old. Everyone – even my mum – has called me Jimmy since the day I was born. We used to live within walking distance of Snapper, but when Dad died, Mum sold the house and moved to Mudgeeraba. I thought it was a dump, but she said it was more like where she came from anyway.

I'm on my way to her now, but first I drop my board into The Horse's to get the ding repaired. I'm still fuming. As always, The Horse demands to know what happened. He has a good laugh at my story, his messed-up tombstone teeth poking out through his rubbery purple lips. It lightens my mood a bit, even though he quotes me sixty bucks. They reckon The Horse must be a millionaire, he fixes that many boards, but I'm fucked if I know what he does with his money because his house is a shithole. In the yard there's wrecked cars and piles of timber and bloody, fly flecked fish bins. Heaped high against the house are a thousand sacks of fuck-knows-what, all beginning to split at the seams. There's even a child's buggy, but he doesn't have a missus, let alone a kid. Everywhere – even on the roof – there are empty 4X cans.

The Horse has never surfed a day in his life, and doesn't have the slightest interest in it, but he's a magician when it comes to fixing a board. If you ding your board within the first six months of owning it – when you're still precious about it – he's the only man for the job.

I leave the board with The Horse, who says he'll have it done in a couple of days, then drive the twenty minutes to Mudgeeraba. I know Mum will offer to make me breakfast but it's always fucking porridge and I can't stand it. I get a pie at the servo instead. I scoff it down because it's only lukewarm, and there's more gristle than meat.

As I pull into the driveway, I see Mum talking to Bruce the neighbour over the fence. Since his wife died last year, she talks to him a lot. I tease her that she spends more time leaning on that fence than she does on her walker.

"Hello, love," she says as I get out of the car. "You're up early. Been surfing?"

"Sort of," I reply.

Bruce gives me a nod and goes back inside, and I hold Mum's elbow as she goes up the ramp to the house. She concentrates fiercely as she goes – the walking frame leads, her good leg next and the bad one dragging behind. The thick sole on her shoe has worn down on one side.

The house is as neat as a pin, apart from a single mug on the kitchen table. I wonder what she thinks about each morning as she sits there drinking her tea. Me, probably.

Both my mum and dad came from Irish backgrounds, but my mum never got the memo that she was supposed to have loads of kids, so there's just my sister Rachel and me. Rachel's only two years older than I am, but in life she's streets ahead. When we were at school it was predestined to be the other way around; I was the bright one, the doctor, the lawyer. She left school as early as she could and got work in a hairdresser's, purely so that she could afford to leave home. She went from sweeping up the hair to cutting it in less than three months. Within three years she'd bought the salon from the owner. One day she cut the hair of a young banker and now they have three girls. He was from Mud, but they moved to Broadbeach and then to the waterways at Macintosh Island as he got bigger and bigger pay rises. She sold the salon and got a heap of cash for that, too. It's basically what happened to my mum, but in reverse.

Mum and I sit in the kitchen for a while, drinking mugs of tea. Her cup says 'World's Best Mum' on the front, and I spin it around so it's facing her.

"Are you, though?" I say, tapping the mug. "Prove it."

She smiles and offers me porridge.

She has this look, my mum, like she's worn out by life. It's like a mixture of plain wrecked-tired and resignation that her lot is not quite what she'd paid for, but there's fuck all she can do about it. She looks defeated, broken by the hand she's been dealt.

Mum asks me to cut the grass, so I wheel the lawnmower out of the garage and fire it up. There are long tufts where the sprinkler has strayed, but the rest's more stones and dirt than grass. Clouds of dust rise into the air.

When I'm done, I wheel the mower back into the garage and pause in the silence to wipe the sweat off my brow. Dad's tools are on the workbench, and there's a tub of old rags, on top of which I recognise strips of his old Broncos T-shirt.

All of a sudden I'm sixteen again, and it's my birthday. I'm out of the house early and into my wettie, and I'm walking down beside the garage to get my board and I see through the grimy garage window my dad wearing that same T-shirt, and he's passed out in the shitty old armchair he dragged in there so that he can sit in it and drink all night. There are cans all over the table and his usual Jim Beam bottle lying empty on the floor. He had his mates with him last night when I went to bed, but now he's on his own. I quietly stand in the doorway and stare at him, hate sizzling in my head.

There are two unopened cans of 4X on the floor beside his chair and I sneak in to get them and it's then that I twig he isn't snoring – he usually sounds like a pig gorging from a trough. I get the cans and straighten up to look at his face. He's a shade of purple, and stone-still, and straightaway I know he's dead.

The stillness and silence are suddenly so deep that I'm overawed by it, like you get when you walk into an empty church. I'm not afraid. The hate's replaced with a kind of wonder. I've wanted to kill him so many times, but now he's gone and done the job himself. Walls topple. Possibilities stretch in all directions. I stare at him for a long time and watch as a fly walks around on his face, stopping at the moisture of his lips.

Finally I tear myself away from his face. There's a pack of cigs on the table and I check if there are any left. Nothing. I think about checking his pockets for money but I don't want to touch him and there'll be fuck-all anyway. The thought occurs to me that I'd only be stealing from my mum now too.

I take the two 4Xs and stash them under the garage, then grab my board and jog to the beach.

I remember the surf that morning – small and razor-edged, machine-cut, a stiff offshore sending a fine spray from the falling lip of each wave. The older guys were struggling, I remember, but I must have weighed sixty kilos and I was as quick to my feet as I've ever been before or since. Up the point they snaked and jostled and pushed each other too deep, and I waited until they inevitably couldn't make the section and dropped in. I got a bucketload of waves, tearing along the green walls and folding myself into the smallest of barrels which seemed to spin forever.

I didn't think about my dad once that morning as I rode those waves. What I remember most was the weightlessness, the freedom. I can still see the extraordinary colour of everything – cerise dawn and then golden sunlight; straw-hued sand; water turning from copper to a thousand shades of blue as the sun rose; foam as white as snow. It had a clarity I hadn't noticed before, a vividness that seemed brand new.

I roll the mower under the workbench and sweep out the garage. I open the lid of the wheelie bin. In a week Mum's produced so little rubbish that it doesn't seem worth bringing it out to the gate, but I do it anyway.

These are my Sundays and I know I'm a sad fuck. I should have been lying in bed with Jess all morning, then heading out for brunch with the rest of the hungover crew and then on to Sunday arvo drinks. But I walk back inside and see my mum's little back hunched over the sink and her hand, white-knuckled, gripping her walker and I see the ham sandwiches under the gauze cloth on the table and I know that I'm stuck.

Chapter 4

It's almost five o'clock when I go to leave. Mum wants me to stay for dinner but it's stew and I've had enough stew to last me a lifetime. She's set for the week – I've done her shopping and stuck it all in the fridge. I vacuumed the lounge and her bedroom and swept and mopped the kitchen floor. I checked the batteries in her panic pager even though they were fresh last Sunday. We had an argument when I saw that she'd lifted the phone back up onto the table in the hallway from the little chair I'd placed it on. She told me not to worry, that it wouldn't happen again, but I still remember the gasping, breathy whistle that I listened to for so long before I even realised it was her. She'd fallen, and it had taken her three hours to drag herself to the hallway where she'd tugged at the phone cord until it fell on top of her and she was able to make the call. I still remember seeing her lying there on the carpet, soaked in her own piss.

On the way back I decide to call over to Jess. She'll be back from the pub and making her dinner and I'm feeling a bit hollow and I don't want to go back to my flat.

It's getting dark as I reach her house and I park on the roadside. I peer into the gloom because I think I can see Willo's car down the street driving away from me but I can't be sure.

I go around to Jess's back door but I can't see her through the kitchen window. I knock gently and let myself in and she's not in the kitchen or the lounge so I call out to her.

There's a sort of a yelp from the bedroom and some thumping sounds and she calls back to me.

"Hey Jimmy," she says. "I'm on the loo – be out in a minute."

But I go into her bedroom and I see her unmade bed and I walk over to the doorway to the ensuite. She's naked, sitting on the dunny, and she smiles up at me. She looks a bit drunk and her hair's untied and messy.

"Hi. How's your mum?" she asks, not looking at me, unwinding toilet paper from the roll.

"OK," I say. "She wants to see you."

Jess nods, looks down at the floor.

"I'm going to shower," she says, but when she gets up from the toilet I put my arms around her waist and lift her up like a caveman and carry her back to the bed and drop her onto it. I grunt at her, paw at her breasts with my knuckles. But she's not playing. She rolls away from me.

"Were you sleeping?" I ask, and she murmurs yes, but I'm thinking she doesn't look like she was. I lie down beside her and we're still for a while, saying nothing. She's warm and soft and my hand is resting in the curve of her waist and then I'm grabbing her arse but without a word she rolls out of the other side of the bed and walks back to the ensuite and turns on the shower.

I lie there, thinking, the sound of the water splashing in the silence. When she gets out I'm going to ask her if she's OK, if there's anything wrong. She showers for a long time, and when she finally comes back into the bedroom, her hair wrapped in a towel, and another around her body, I don't ask her what's wrong. I ask her where she went for a drink and who was there.

"Cove Bar. Sal, Ginny, Suze and Scott, Amy, Brett."

"Willo?" I say.

"Oh yeah, him too," she says. She turns away and pulls the towel off her head and dries her hair again. It doesn't need drying again.

"Anyone drink too much?" I ask.

"Yeah, me," she replies, and she laughs, but she doesn't smile.

"How'd you get home?" I say, and when she tells me that Willo dropped her off I don't reply. I just stand up and walk out.

Chapter 5

I get the first call from Willo the next morning at smoko. I'm outside the house I'm working in, sitting in the sun on the step, drinking tea and eating a Gingernut. I'm buggered – it must have been four in the morning when I finally fell asleep.

The old lady inside made me the tea but I know she'd rather I finished tiling her bathroom and fucked off; she keeps poking her head around the door to see if I'm working. I don't blame her – my phone pinged so many times this morning that I put it on silent. Texts from Jess, but I haven't read any of them.

I've no intention of answering the phone, but suddenly a hot squirt of anger pulses through me and I decide I want to hear what the arsehole has to say.

"Willo," I say.

"How're ya, Jimmy," he replies. "You working?"

"Yep."

There's a pause. He's shitting himself.

"Good weekend?" he asks. The fucker's trying to find out if I know.

"It was all right. You?"

"Just the usual," he says.

"Yeah? Did you have fun last night?" I ask. I can't keep the edge out of my voice.

"Yeah, pub was good. We missed you."

Fuck you Willo.

"How about after the pub?"

"Jimmy…" he starts, but he tails off.

"What?"

"I'm sorry, mate," he says, but I don't hear the rest because I hang up.

I get back to work and don't stop for lunch. I tell the old bird that if she's OK with it I'll just keep going until I'm done. Of course she is, and I work as fast as I can, finishing the grouting about six. I wipe it all clean and ask to borrow her vacuum cleaner to tidy up but she says she'll do it.

She gives me cash, counting it all out painfully into my hand like it's my pocket money. I chuck it in the glove box and drive straight to D-Bah. The sun's on the horizon already but I need to get in the water.

The sea breeze has died away but the waves are still mush. There's only a handful out. I spot the odd one creaming off the rocks and drag out my old Parsons fish from its cover and it's while I'm rubbing wax on it that I start to cry. I keep my head down and keep on waxing until I'm angry again and I stop blubbing.

By the time I paddle out there's less than fifteen minutes of light left. I half-heartedly stroke into a few but I end up just sitting on my board and staring at the horizon until it gets dark.

When I come in, I sit in the car reading Jess's texts. The first ones came through last night and the last one just a few minutes ago. I scroll back to the start, and as I read through them I can see the progression – innocence, confusion, denial, guilt and now grovelling. Willo must have called her because after lunch there's nothing but pleading and excuses.

A part of me must have clung on to the hope that I'd been mistaken, that it wasn't Willo's car disappearing down the street and that he'd been about to apologise for something else. I cry again, and pound the steering wheel with both hands.

I start to work all the hours god sends. I start work in yet another brand-new, shitty high-rise hotel at Surfers and I tile three bathrooms in a week and the foreman can't believe his luck. Says I can have all the work I want. I'm getting dirty looks from the other tilers but I ignore them. I'm eating Chinese and Korean and Vietnamese takeaways every night straight out of the tub and then just going to bed, where I toss and turn all night. By now I've had calls from Sal, Scott and Brett but I don't answer any of them. Someone knocks on the door early Friday evening but I don't answer it.

The waves are good on Saturday morning and there's a guilt-ridden text from Willo to meet for a surf, but I go straight back to the hotel and start on another bathroom. On Sunday I go around to Mum's.

Rachel and the kids are there and we all have lunch together and when they leave I tell Mum about Jess and Willo. She's shocked, uncomprehending. She doesn't understand how young people can do this to each other. She says it's like one of those crappy reality TV shows. She's madder at Willo than she is at Jess, but then she's known Willo for twenty years. It's questionable whether over the course of his life he's spent more time in his house or ours. His dad was even shittier than mine, and he basically lived with us until Mum sent him home each night.

I listen to her giving out and I realise I'm numb. I've worked myself to a standstill, hardly slept and now I can barely concentrate on what she's saying. She's trying to make me feel better, to let me know that I'm not to blame, but it only makes me feel worse. I can't listen to it any more. Rachel went shopping for her and she's all set for the week, and so I stand up, kiss her on the forehead and walk out. She follows me out, shuffling along on her walking frame, and stands on the porch as I get into my car. It's not your fault, she tells me.

I don't start the car. I just sit there staring at Mum for a while. I don't even wind down my window. I'm suddenly furious with her and I want to get out of the car and scream at her that it's her fucking fault. She took all the beatings and abuse from Dad for years and didn't say or do shit. He punctured her lung and broke her ribs and mashed up her face too many times to remember anything other than the constant purple-yellow-black aftermath of it, there more often than not. He dislocated her shoulder and busted her leg and crippled her for life and she just fucking took it and stayed put and I know if I got out of the car right now and asked her why she'd say she did it for Rachel and me. And because of that I'm here minding her and not at the fucking pub with my mates and her shitty cowardice is the reason I wasn't there to stop what was going on with Jess and Willo. It's the reason I settled for a job staring at bathroom walls all day. She never said shit when I got the apprenticeship; she told me she was happy for me, rather than saying I was making a big mistake and should be going to university instead like I was supposed to do.

'It's your fucking fault', I mouth to Mum through the car window, but she thinks I'm saying something nice to her and she blows me a kiss. Like a fucking pussy I do nothing, say nothing, just start the car and back out of the driveway.

I lie on my bed for the rest of the afternoon, staring at the ceiling. I'm connecting the shitty dots in my life and stringing them together in different ways. Mum's off the hook now; mostly I'm blaming myself.

Eventually I'm driven back out by hunger and I order fried rice from the Chinese takeaway on the corner and try to ignore the dead flies on the windowsill while I wait for it. I sit on the park bench across the road and eat half it out of the tub but there's something putrid in it; some sour vegetable taste and I sling the rest into the rubbish bin. On the way home I get a bottle of Bundy and two litres of Coke from the offy. There's no ice in my freezer so I just drink it warm from a coffee mug because the glasses are too small for this job. I drink fast, cup after cup, and after a while I turn off the telly and the lights and open the sliding door and sit in the opening staring out into the dark. A thousand moths have gathered around a streetlight, all clattering around each other in an idiotic, futile dance.

The next morning I wake with a filthy head. I could take the morning off but I know I'm never going to get back to sleep anyway so I get up. The chemical smell on my breath and body are toxic as fuck even after I get out of the shower.

It occurs to me while I'm in the queue at the Macca's drive-through that I'd still be way over the limit and shouldn't be driving, so I order two sausage McMuffins and a hash brown and sit in the carpark and force it all down. The coffee is nasty, acidic, but maybe it's just the state of my guts. I'm hit with a fierce indigestion almost immediately, and my head is lifting so I stop again to get a bottle of water and Panadol from the servo. I drive the rest of the way to the hotel, burping and regurgitating my breakfast in tiny, burning spews.

It's well after nine when I get to work. I'm in the lift when my phone rings and it's Rachel. For a moment I'm confused because it doesn't sound like her, but then I realise that she's crying and her breath is coming in jerky, ragged sobs.

"Jesus. Rachel? What's wrong?"

"Jimmy," she says, but it's more like an anguished moan than a word. Then there's a long silence as she's swallowing and trying to pull herself together and into it my stomach falls and I can feel a sort of electrical fizzing in my head.

"Rachel, here, give it to me," I hear my brother-in-law Gus say, and he comes on the line.

"Jimmy, you there, mate?" Gus doesn't sound right either, his voice pitching higher than usual.

"What, Gus, what is it?"

"It's your mum, Jimmy," he says, as Rachel howls in the background.

Chapter 6

Rachel and me are sitting in the bedroom with Mum and we hear the doorbell ring and Gus's deep voice greeting people in the hallway. It's all about to kick off and this is probably going to be our last moments alone with Mum. Rachel smiles at me and puts out her hand and I take it and we stand together looking down into the coffin like little kids. The undertaker's done her best; her head isn't swollen anymore, but there's no hiding the graze on the side of her face.

She looks peaceful but also a bit weird, her face manipulated by the undertaker into an expression I've never seen before. The wrinkles around her lips and corners of her eyes have been smoothed out somehow and it's taken years off her – Rachel and me were laughing about it last night. She's wearing a white cotton nightie that Rachel picked out and it suits her. Surrounded by the satin folds of the coffin, she could be lying on some fancy hotel bed.

Rachel bends to kiss her and then goes out into the hallway to Gus, closing the door behind her. I stand there in the silence, and I can't stop thinking about how I buggered off on her on Sunday, how angry I was. I remember glancing back at her from the road before I drove away, and it only comes to me now how small she looked, how frail and shaky, her tiny arms gripping her walking frame. How long after I left was it before she caught the edge of the walker on the door frame and pitched forward, the crown of her head thumping against the fridge? Was she knocked out immediately, or was she conscious, lying over the top of her walker, the circulation to the lower half of her body slowly being cut off? How long did it take her to die?

I bend and press my forehead to her hands, which are clasped together, her string of rosary beads wound between her fingers. They're cold and hard and still as stones, but I keep my head there and tell her I'm sorry.

The kitchen is full of people and noise, and plates of egg sandwiches and carrot cake and pikelets are already spreading towards the edges of the table. Gus is making tea as fast as he can, and I realise that I forgot to get extra milk. But Gus is on it and has already sent the girls to the shop on the corner.

I shake the hands of lots of people I know and some I don't, and in dribs and drabs they take turns to go into Mum's room to pay their respects and say goodbye. People turn up in their droves to Irish wakes, Mum once told me, and she's right. Everyone from her hairdresser to the Indian guy who runs the fruit store drops in, and there's a core crowd that stays after the hearse takes her off to the undertaker's for the night. Gus produces a slab of beer and four bottles of wine and we drag out plastic chairs from the garage and I make a bench from a scaffolding board and some breeze blocks and we sit around outside and talk and drink and eat the rest of the Cheerios and sangers. I think it's going to be shit and I want them all to go home but in spite of myself I start to feel better. Mum's mates are sad but they're awful funny and the stories are flowing and they're laughing like drainpipes. Some of the tales they tell about Mum sound like they're about someone else and they laugh at my goggle-eyed disbelief.

Everyone shoots off home about ten and I roll into bed. I've drunk away my hangover but I'm dog-tired. To my surprise I sleep like a baby and the next morning I wake up so late that I've only just got time to shower, scoff some Cornflakes and I'm into my number ones and out the door and heading for the church.

It's not until I'm listening to Mum's best friend talking about her up there at the pulpit that it hits me that I'm actually here, saying goodbye to my mother. When I glance at Rachel and see the pain etched on her face I can't help it anymore and I start to cry, tears rolling down my cheeks and making little dark patches on my shirt. I lean forward and cover my face with my hands and when I feel my youngest niece gently touch my back to comfort me it makes me cry even more. Images of my mother pulse through my mind. I see her apologising for not making my footy matches because her face was rearranged by Dad the night before. I see her in the morning, praying the rosary, the pot of tea at her elbow ghosting vapour into the sunlit stillness. Dad ruled the evenings, but the mornings were ours – Mum's and Rachel's and mine. I'd get up earlier than Rachel to have Mum to myself for a little while. I see ten thousand meals, a mountain of ironed T-shirts and shorts, an ocean of soapy water and dishes.

Jess sits with the rest of my mates – Willo included – near the back of the church and afterwards, outside, they come up in a line and hug me one by one. Jess whispers 'I'm sorry' into my ear and she smells beautiful and I don't want to let her go but she's already moving away. I can see Willo's been crying but he can't look me in the eye and he hugs me quickly and walks away without saying anything.

Only the family and the priest go to the graveyard and it's a short ceremony. The girls have picked flowers and the petals flutter down onto the coffin after it's lowered into the ground and they're crying as they throw them. Our handfuls of red earth clatter on to the lid. Then it's over, and the gravedigger pulls a sheet of fake grass over the hole.

We go back to the RSA for a cup of tea and something to eat. Mum went there to have her dinner every Thursday for the past ten years and they won't hear of charging us for the food. There's lots of people, and I catch myself searching for Jess but I can't see her or any of my friends and I'm relieved. Cups of tea turn to pints of beer and there are more stories and one of Mum's mates gets me in a corner and tells me how sorry she was that she didn't help us out more; she should have gone to the cops and pushed my mum harder to leave the old bastard.

We finish at about eight and go back to the house. We clean up a bit and then suddenly Gus and the girls are in the car waiting for Rachel. She grabs my arms and holds me in front of her, staring into my face.

She asks if I'm OK and I nod and tell her I think so. After all the noise and people I'm stunned by the silence and I don't know if I like it or not.

"I want you to have the house," she says to me, and I go to protest but she shakes her head and insists. "We don't bloody need it, do we? Do what you want with it. You could live in it or sell it – whatever you think. Please Jimmy, you deserve it. Mum would have wanted you to have it."

Rachel hugs me and gets into the car and I smile at the girls in the back seat as they pull away. I go back into the house and the quiet is so deep it's like a solid thing and now I know I can't stand it. I cover my face and arms with mozzie repellent and get a sleeping bag from the hall cupboard which I roll out on the bench seat on the porch. Out here there's some noise; the hum and whir of insects, the hiss of distant traffic on the motorway. I imagine the long exhalation of some giant and ferocious animal, exhausted from a day spent ripping the world apart. I cocoon myself in the sleeping bag, pulling it over my head.

Chapter 7

It takes just a couple of weeks to sell the house. I stayed there for two days painting the lounge and Mum's room and trying to figure out if I could live in it or not, but I pretty much knew from the start that I couldn't. The real estate agent is a slimy wanker and I know fuck-all about the process and it all seems suspiciously quick to me. He shakes my hand with his cold-fish grip and presents me with a cheque for $345,900. I know it's less than it should be, but it's still a shitload of money to me.

I call Rachel and tell her, trying to talk her into accepting half but she won't hear of it and she doesn't want to know what I got for the house. Says it's my business.

I deposit the money in my bank account and go back to work. I work Saturdays and Sundays, sometimes for longer hours than I do during the week. I'm keeping the Queensland takeaway industry alive, eating whatever shit food is closest. Every now and again I go to one of those vegan cafés where everyone's wearing yoga pants and I buy the biggest salad on the menu in an attempt to restore some sort of order to my insides.

Jess texts me every day and tries to call a bunch of times, and one day when I'm sitting in my car on the esplanade, I answer. She's so surprised that she doesn't speak for a moment, but then she's babbling, apologising and crying and saying what an awful mistake she's made. We talk for forty minutes, and I oscillate between feeling numb, like I'm overhearing someone else's conversation, and stabbing jolts of pure anger. I demand to know what they did, her and Willo, and how many times. She doesn't want to tell me but I scream at her and she tells me, crying her heart out. It slices into me, that information, and I'm so hurt and angry that I hang up on her and eventually switch off my phone to stop her from calling.

That night when I get home I'm restless as fuck and I go back out to the offy and they've only got the 700ml size of Bundy so I get two of them. This time I get ice and Coke and when I get back I get stuck into it. The first bottle's gone in under two hours and I open the second. I barely feel it.

I get a text from Willo. He's been sending me one every couple of days asking if I want to go surfing like it's the only thing he can think of to do. He's driving up the coast in the morning. I don't reply. I keep drinking and finally it's starting to knock me sideways. I get up for a piss and I have to lean on the wall to stop from lurching about. I catch sight of myself in the mirror and I stand there, swaying slightly. I'm wearing nothing but my old shorts and I can see that my gut has grown a bit over the past few weeks. I suddenly get an awful premonition standing there looking at myself. It might as well be my dad looking back at me, drunk and in his shorts. I lurch away and go back to my glass of Bundy, disgusted.

When I wake in the morning I'm fucked. I stagger to the toilet and spew into it in wracking, violent spasms, the bile tearing at my throat. I vomit for a long time, my guts emptying until there's nothing but yellow scum which I can't seem to rid my mouth of. For the next three hours it's the same, dragging myself to the dunny, retching my ring up and wobbling back to bed again. I don't even call in sick. I can barely get to the kitchen for water.

The tide finally turns at about one-ish, and I'm well enough to prop myself up on my pillow. My phone's on the bedside table. Unlocking the screen, I'm surprised to see that I'm three-quarters of the way through making a Garuda Airways booking to Bali for next week. I have absolutely no memory of it. I lie there staring at it for a long time. Then I roll out of bed to find my passport.

Chapter 8

The day before I leave, I pick up my last wage packet from the foreman and then go around to my sister's to have lunch with her and the girls. Rachel's got this look on her face like I'm making a mistake and I feel like a child being told off even though she says nothing. The girls make a fuss of me and it strikes me that they love me out of all proportion to the time I spend with them. I know that it's because my sister is always talking me up to them and they're not old enough not to believe her. I'm thankful for it.

As we're sitting around the table on the deck, the light starts to change, softening and tinting deeper. We all look up and it takes a while to realise that it's smoke from the inland bushfires that have been raging all week. A wind change has turned the giant pall and sent it out over the coast.

As I drive back to my flat it gets deeper and by the time I'm in the taxi heading to the airport it's a sickly yellow filter making the world look freakishly apocalyptic. It carries the weird unease of an eclipse. I've seen it before, but it's a surprise each time how it affects me. I'm ill-at-ease, fearful. It turns my thoughts against me; it's a bad omen, I'm making a mistake. I sit in silence and my monosyllabic answers to the taxi driver soon shut him up. I close my eyes to block out the awful light until we get to the airport and I hurry inside like a troglodyte into the safety of his cave.

As soon as I get to Bali I know I'm not going to stay long. My mates have all been here heaps of times and they never stop raving about it, but I instantly take a dislike to it. I see the elaborate architecture and the mysterious Hindu temples, but I can't separate them from the mosaic of litter, the plastic bags drifting on the wind and the intermittent wafting stench of sewage. Black smoke rises from behind walls and I see rats hurrying along the tops. In the morning the locals are out everywhere with brooms sweeping out the gated compounds and walled gardens, but they're only pushing it around and the shit gathers in the drains and the alleyways and it feels like they're sweeping their whole lives under the carpet. I see it all up close because the traffic is gridlocked the whole way.

Worst of all are the thousands of Aussies and Brits and Germans everywhere, their fat arses stuffed into cossies and T-shirts too small for them, their tattooed skin sweaty and sunburned. It's still early when I arrive but already they're thick through Kuta, hassling street vendors for bargains, going for a cure in the bars. I see the odd magic mushy casualty from the night before staring into space or vomiting into the gutter. I see a white girl curled up on the footpath whose hair looks like it's been pulled out; chunks of it are missing and I can see the white of her scalp.

They don't give a fuck about anything but themselves, these people. They arrive, take a shit on the place, and leave.

I was going to stop in Kuta for a night but I'm sickened by it and I tell the taxi driver to keep going. The traffic's awful the whole way, and it takes forty-five minutes to get out along the

Bukit Peninsula to the top of the cliff at Bingin. I pay the driver and get out and I'm swamped by Balinese – from little kids to old ladies – all wanting to carry my board bag and backpack down the cliff. I'm a bit freaked and I walk past them all and start down the stairs. Half of them follow me, jabbering in my ear about the deals at their losmens. I remember someone telling me that Bingin was pretty basic but my information is clearly old because I can see fancy resorts and guest houses everywhere. I see three ding repair stalls and there's a surf shop near the top of the cliff.

It's only after I check into the shittiest losmen on the beach that it occurs to me that I should have chosen something flasher. The foreman at the Surfers hotel handed me twelve grand yesterday. But it's clean and tidy and there's a bar that looks out over the ocean. I have a room to myself and I can see a monkey sitting in the tree outside it.

The tide is full, and mushy swells are capping and foaming along the reef and there's only a couple of paddle boarders out. Apparently yesterday was all-time, but to me it still looks promising – it's over head-high and the wind is non-existent. The ocean's a glossy sheet of ultramarine blue.

It's almost midday and I order a nasi goreng and a smoothie and sit in the restaurant. A couple of Aussie girls are lounging on couches and half a dozen European backpackers are playing cards and it's pleasant enough. I eat, then go to my room. I lie on my bed and close my eyes.

I can see the reef from my bed, and when I wake I check it straightaway. There's no one out, and I can see that the tide has dropped. The waves are just starting to stand up.

I log into the WiFi and my phone starts pinging. There's a bunch of messages – almost all from Jess. I told her two days ago that I was going, and she begged me not to, wanting to meet me, but I refused. Truth is I'm afraid of what I'll do when I see her – I have no doubt I'll sabotage any chance we might have because anger still seethes through me whenever I think about her and Willo. Every phone call we've had ends with me hanging up, and I know I've only got a couple more of those up my sleeve before she decides that perhaps she won't bother trying to get me back after all. It's a stupid, intricate game of just how much I can punish her and I hate myself for playing it but I can't seem to stop. This trip's part of it – both of us are in no doubt about that. She went silent for a long time when I told her I had an open-ended ticket.

I scroll through her messages – I'm sorry; I love you; have fun; be careful – and I send her one back, a photo of me lying on the bed with the ocean in the background. I look miserable in it, but a smile feels like too much to give her.

There's a text from Willo, and he must have been pissed when he sent it because it's a gushing apology, saying how much he regrets what happened and that he doesn't want to lose me as a mate. I don't finish reading it. I delete it.

I can see a lone paddler heading out to the reef. I watch him for a while and he catches a couple of waves which rear up nicely and maintain form long enough for one turn before fattening out again.

By the time I've screwed my fins into my board and given it a fresh rub of warm water wax there are five guys out and two more on the beach. I can see the take-off zone is tiny and they sit shoulder to shoulder. I start thinking that maybe I should chill for a while and surf after the low tide, but a couple of decent sets come through and a few waves go unridden. I slather suncream all over my face, pull on a rashie and head down to the beach, my board under my arm. It's brand new – another Hammo – his Indo special. I picked it up two days ago and the groms in the shop were jealous as fuck and frothing, asking me about all the places I was going to surf.

As soon as I step onto the sand I see them. A dozen or so surfers all doing the same as me. They're streaming out of their losmens on to the beach like ants and strapping on their leggies.

Some fuckwits are stretching and warming up on the shore like they've got a heat coming up. I spot three paddle boarders walking down the beach towards me.

I stop and stand there, adding them all up. But more and more appear and I sit down on the sand and just watch them. Within half an hour there are thirty-five on the peak, all scrapping and paddling for every chunk of water that passes through. It gets better and better but the crowd's almost as rabid as Snapper. Another half an hour and the Indos start to turn up. There's only five or six of them, but they get every second wave, padding straight to the inside, taking off deeper than anyone and threading the barrel with practised ease. I hear them screaming at anyone daring to paddle for a wave that they deem is theirs, which is pretty much all of them.

I walk back up to my losmen. I stand for a moment on the steps, looking back up the point, but it's too small for Impossibles and I can see a shitload of people already out at Padang.

I go back to my room and jam the new Hammo back into the board bag. Then I go to the bar.

Chapter 9

It's a two-hour ferry trip to G-Land and I feel like shit so I know I'm going to spew the whole way. I'm waiting for the ferry, lying in a heap on the jetty, and when it arrives I talk to two Aussies who've just come back from there. They're rightly pissed off. A shitload of fuckheads from Margaret's showed up three days ago, getting paralytic every night and shitting on everyone in the surf. The crowd was already bad enough before they arrived. They're all there for another ten days because it looks like the swell is going to kick again.

I don't even get on the boat. The guy can't understand it and he's ready to fight with me so he doesn't have to give my money back, but I just walk away and find a quiet bar in Kuta.

I'm six beers in when the Indo dude behind the bar asks if I want to stay upstairs and I agree and drag my shit up to the room but come straight back down to keep drinking. Jess is sending me endless texts but I ignore them all.

There's just me and the barman in the bar and he's trying to be friendly but I can't seem to make the effort to talk to him.

He's looking at me nervously so I leave and wander aimlessly around Kuta. Every twenty seconds a hawker tries to sell me something. A guy offers me weed in an alleyway and I'm tempted but I've heard of those poor fuckers who buy it and the next thing they know they're being arrested and they pay the bribe which is split between the cop and the dealer who takes back the gear and sells it to the next fuckwit stupid enough to buy it. I tell him to fuck off, but he follows me for a while, all teeth and wide eyes and it's hard to tell if he's angry or happy or just mental.

I find another bar that isn't heaving with tourists and I keep going on the Bintangs. By dusk I'm well-oiled, and I get a mee goreng to soak some of it up. But I'm not hungry – at least not for food – and I move on to the spirits, rum and Cokes and tequila. I've moved to another bar and this one is heaving and I'm chatting to a girl who's lost the rest of the hen party but she doesn't seem to care. She wants to dance and I try but I'm too pissed and when she sees me wobbling around she says she's going to the bathroom and doesn't come back.

I leave and go to another bar and it's a riot of disco lights and the bartender offers me a mushroom milkshake and I drink it in one go and then order a whiskey to get rid of the shitty taste. I get up to go for a piss, but somehow I find myself in the back kitchen instead and an old woman doing something to a mountain of chicken carcasses just stares at me silently until I leave again.

I stagger out into the night and decide to go back to the place I'm staying but I'm fucked if I can find the street. It's a circus of fairy lights and loud music and motorbikes and street vendors and it's all starting to vibrate in a new way. Things are further away or closer than they look and I can't tell which is which. Decisions seem important but I can't bring myself to make them. I step between two shops and vomit copiously on to the dirt, and the shopkeepers come out, screaming at me but I lurch away and keep going. I see the darkness of an alleyway and I go for it like a cockroach trying to escape the light. I have to hold onto the walls as I make my way along it, and a dog barks furiously behind a gate. When I get to the other end I see that I've reached the beach and I sink down on the sand and immediately I'm set upon by hawkers but when I spew again they all fuck off. I roll on to my back and lie there, paralysed, the sour smell of vomit in my nostrils and the remains of it burning my throat. The world turns in frightening, paroxysmal circles. I don't know how many more times I spew but it's a lot, and between times I alternate between hyperventilating and trying to hold my breath to stop it. Finally, mercifully, I pass out.

When I wake there are hands holding me down and searching my pockets. Someone kneels hard on my face. I try to fight, but I'm struck on the side of the head with something heavy and it sends sparks across my vision. I'm punched in the ribs viciously again and again and the pain sears immediately through my body. Then they're off me and I think that's it but I get a kick in the head so hard a black halo contracts into my field of vision and I'm suddenly deep in a tunnel looking out towards the entrance. I realise that they're my own ragged gasps in the dark silence afterwards but it sounds like they're coming from someone else. The black corona breathes, swelling and receding, and little smoky wisps dancing around the edges show against the bright streetlights. I've seen this before, I remember, when my father punched me so hard that I suffered from concussion for weeks afterwards. I was twelve. I can see him now, his puce, enraged face bellowing into mine, me frozen to the spot with fear. Like a silent movie it flickers across my vision, then it seems to rewind, to begin over again. I see my mum rushing to help me, then I see how viciously he shoves her. I see her slam into the exposed nogs of the garage and slump on to the floor. Then I go flying, stupefied by the force of his blow, rolling across the concrete floor. I remember lying there looking up at him, and the black mist encroaching from all sides. The panic of experiencing your body do something it's never done before. He was coming at me for more, but somehow my mum's scream reached him, jerking him out of his rage just enough to check himself, and he charged out into the night.

It takes me a long time to get back to my room. It's just beginning to get light but there are plenty of people around, shadowy figures in doorways lit by the glow of cigarettes, and groups of cackling Indo prostitutes walking home. A couple of them peel away from their group to proposition me but when they see my face they turn away without saying anything. I'm driven by an instinct for self-preservation that I didn't seem to possess last night. I can feel the blood matting on my temple and my head pounds in my skull. I'm walking bent over to one side because my ribs hurt so much.

I have to bang on the door of the bar because I've lost the key to my room. At first the guy doesn't recognise me, but he lets me in eventually and follows me through the bar telling me to shower first, and that I have to pay for a new key, and if I ruin the bedsheets I'll have to pay for them too. He tells me I have to pay for another night because he knows there's no way that I'll be making check-out time. I give him the thumbs up as he hands me the spare key and drag myself up to my room. There will be no shower – I can barely stay upright. I grunt in pain as I collapse onto the bed and pass into a nightmarish coma.

Chapter 10

I get the fuck out of Bali and travel steadily north for the next four weeks. I spend a few days at a surf camp at the top of Java, but my ribs are still too sore to surf properly. I think I've fractured one but I don't go to a doctor.

But it slowly mends and I ferry to Sumatra and work my way up the mainland, surfing pretty average Krui, Honeys and Jimmy's. I take a boat to Banana Island. It's still early in the season but I get a decent swell when I get to the Ments but it's as crowded as fuck. I stay three days at Hollow Trees before I move on. I don't bother with Nias – I've seen the videos and I run into pissed-off surfers everywhere who say you sit for an hour between each wave to snag one from the pros.

I hate the surf camps more and more. At first I'm mesmerised by the scenery and the set-up, but I notice the way the Indos look at the surfers and I know they can't stand us but they grovel around trying to please just the same. And wherever I go mongrel Aussies spend the night necking Bintangs and spewing and wrestling with each other while the Indos stand around with waxen grins on their faces, but I know given half a chance they'd just as soon take to them with their machetes. The surf camps are usually run by some American or Aussie societal dropout with a submissive Indo wife and a drinking problem, and they're used to ordering staff around and treating them like shit.

If an Indo's income isn't directly reliant on tourists their hostility is naked and serious, and twice I get into standoffs with boat skippers who decide to charge me more once we're at sea than what we agreed upon on land. I argue for a bit, but in their position I'd probably do the same so I hand over the cash. I see surfers with black eyes and fat lips after tangling with the locals and it's probably all over ten bucks.

The best surf I get is on Simeulue – perfect six-foot A-frames with a short, sharp hollow left and a long right-hander with two barrel sections. There are six guys on it when I paddle out: five mates from Spain or somewhere in South America, whose lives seem to depend on catching every wave, and one Brazilian who ruins the Brazo stereotype by acting like a gentleman. The Spanish boys don't even nod in my direction, but the Brazo strikes up a conversation. He's travelling alone like me.

I snaffle a few warm-up waves that slide underneath the crew, but now I'm hungry for one of the bombs. I take my place at the back of the queue and sit patiently until they've all caught one. Two of the Spanish lads are back out again and there's one either side of me and I can't believe it when they both paddle with intent when the next wave rears. I let the guy inside take it, and when I come over the wave a grin spreads over my face because the second wave in the set's an absolute smoker. It's a foot bigger and I'm flat to my board and racing for it and it's close but I turn and I've got time for two good strokes before I'm falling with the lip in a welter of spray. But my feet plant firmly and I stick the drop, skittering out into the flat. Then I'm away and it's a thing of rare beauty, a moving wall of molten glass. It's so smooth and transparent that I can see every piece of coral racing past beneath me, warping and looming as the wave sucks water off the reef. For a few seconds I stand straight and try to take it all in, to imprint this moment on my memory. I know it's an awful cliché, but everything is forgotten and forgiven; it's a sublime suspension of reality, a forceful evacuation of all the shit in my head.

The first barrel section is so beautifully telegraphed that I can see it coming for miles and it's like surfing in slow motion, there's that much time to set up for it. I fade a little and draw out a bottom turn, then put on the brakes with a mid-face check. I slide my front foot to the rail and it all feels automatic, thoughtless. The back door looms.

When the guy paddling back out turns and strokes into my wave down the line I can't quite believe what I'm seeing. The wave throws and I'm as deep as I've ever been in a tube but he's already collapsed the end section and it's all over before it begins. I want to skewer the prick on the end of my board but I'm flicked up and over the falls with an awful violence and I come down hard, driven to the bottom where I hit the reef. I'm pinned for a second and then dragged over the coral on my hip and arse.

It's a long time before I surface in the spritzing foam and I've got just a few seconds before I'm hit with the next wave and then the next. I end up in the shallows, bumping over the coral on my guts and it takes an age to get back out to the channel where I try to assess the damage. My boardies are shredded and my hip stings. Looking down I can see a pink bloom of blood under the water. It's when I sit up on my board that I see the crease right across its deck.

My rage rises like a Mentos tossed into a Coke. I paddle flat out until I reach him, sitting with his mates. They're smiling and laughing and taking the piss, but when I paddle inside their circle, straight up to the guy who dropped in on me they all fall silent. I sit up on my board.

"What the fuck is wrong with you?" I begin, and I see his face harden.

"What?" he says. He tilts his head back, juts out his chin.

"Don't drop in on me, you fuckwit!" I scream, and I take a swing at him.

A fight in the water is never pretty and this is no exception. I hit him but there's no power in it and it ends up as a breath-holding battle as we wrestle each other under the water. But I'm already puffing hard from my furious paddle out and in thirty seconds I'm seeing stars and when he finally lets me go I'm almost drowned and I grovel away holding onto my board and sucking in lungfuls and coughing up water. One of his mates paddles over and punches me in the face and there's nothing I can do about it. Blood's pouring from my nose and it's taking everything I've got just to hang on to my board. A big set washes through and I can't duck-dive or even haul myself on to my board and I just have to take it on the head. I feel weaker every time I come up and it takes me longer each time to reel in my board by the leggie. When my feet touch the bottom they're sliced up on the coral but I have to stand because I can't stay afloat any longer.

It takes me fifteen minutes to reach the beach and I crawl up it, my board dragging along behind me. I keep going until I find shade and lie there for a long time, coughing and retching. When I can get to my feet I stagger up the sand unsteadily, and the Indo lady cleaning out the toilet block gives a little scream when she sees me. I have blood all down my front from my nose and down my leg from the deep cuts on my hip and arse. She runs off in the direction of the kitchen and comes back with Andy, who runs the place.

The next half hour is spent trying not to scream as he squeezes lime juice on the cuts and sticks a dressing over it. Then I spend the rest of the night in my room and leave early the next morning.

I go back to the mainland and catch a bus to Banda Aceh. I can only sit on one arse cheek and it's agony. The blood has seeped through my shorts by the time I find a dodgy hotel, and I try to hide it from the woman at reception. I stay there for a couple of days, doing nothing but reading books, changing the dressing and going out to eat. Banda Aceh's a shithole, but I like that I don't see any tourists until I'm forced to find a four-star hotel in order to get a beer. You can't wear shorts without pissing off the locals, so I buy a pair of cotton trousers and wear them all the time despite the stifling heat.

One evening I'm online and I start poking around trying to find information about the Andamans. I spend half an hour on my phone, endlessly watching a 2002 YouTube video called *Surfing the Andaman Islands* and trying to figure out where it is. The vid is of a bunch of mates on a boat trip who seem to be more interested in fishing, but there's a grainy segment in the middle of the video featuring the best righthander I've ever seen. The boys are obviously out of their league because there's no footage of them riding it, but it grinds down the reef with a precision that's hard to credit. The barrel is square and doesn't pinch and there are no apparent sections. I read all the comments, and some reckon it's Kumari Point, and others say it's been destroyed by the Boxing Day tsunami, but it smacks of the classic surfers' ploy to throw people off the scent. I try to ignore the comment about salt water crocs eating people in the lineup.

There's no flight from Banda Aceh to Port Blair except via Sri Lanka. I can't face travelling south again, so I decide fuck it and book a flight to Colombo where I spend a few days in swanky hotels sitting by the pool. One day I get off my arse and visit the national park in the middle of the country, and the next I travel back to the coast. My cuts have healed enough to get back in the water and I head for Arugam Bay. I'm not expecting much and I don't get it – just a dribbly three foot wave that doesn't have enough power to match the speed at which it breaks. It's crowded and filthy and frustrating, both in and out of the water.

But now I'm hell-bent on getting to the Andaman Islands and I find a guy online called Brian who agrees to take me on his boat so I book a flight to Port Blair. It's the beginning of March and he tells me it's just starting to kick off over there and it sounds like bullshit but he says the magic words – 'few crowds' – and I can't help myself.

I have to fly to Chennai first but I don't give a shit because it's paradise to sit in an air-conditioned space drinking Bloody Marys and watching movies.

I spend the afternoon in Port Blair getting every permit under the sun, and the next morning I get a tuk-tuk to the docks and I find Brian whose schooner looks like it's seen better days. He's loading cases of beer and bottles of spirits on board. His eyes are bloodshot and he looks crazy and when he shakes my hand he stinks of piss.

Brian tells me we're waiting on some others, and when they arrive I make up my mind there and then. A dozen surfers pour out of tuk-tuks and I can see one of them holding money out to the driver and then pulling it back again as he goes to take it. The rest are laughing at the show and one of them is filming it on his phone. It goes on and on until the driver gets fucked off and gets out of his tuk-tuk and yells at him. He hands over the money, but when the driver turns around the guy kicks him up the arse and they all laugh again.

I pick up my board bag and my pack and walk off, and I can hear Brian yelling something to me about money. I'm away down the dock and he doesn't chase me, so I sit down on my pack and I see the schooner cast off and putter out of the harbour. I can see the goons already drinking beer on the back deck. Brian sees me and gives me the finger and his crew all do the same, and then they're gone around the breakwater. I sit there for a while, chucking stones into the water and watching the local fishermen piling nets in heaps on the dock.

After a while a boy approaches and says something but he doesn't speak English and he disappears again. In a few minutes he's back with his father and together they squat beside me. The father's not old, but his leathery face tells of years at sea.

He's smoking a bidi, which he pulls out to grin at me. There's barely a tooth left in his head.

"American?" says the father.

"Aussie," I reply, and the father starts beaming.

"Ah, gidday mate!" he says, laughing and nudging his son.

"Gidday," I say.

"You surfer man?

I nod.

"You go surf them?" he says, pointing at the ocean in the direction the schooner has gone.

"No. Not them. On my own," I say.

He nods and says something to his son.

"You want boat?" he says.

I think for a moment. I know he doesn't have the first inkling about surfing.

"Nah," I say, shaking my head.

I head back to my hotel.

Chapter 11

The next morning I'm back down at the dock but there's no sign of the boy or his father. I pull out a book, sit down and wait.

I spent an hour on Google Maps last night going around and around the coast of Little Andaman and I think I've narrowed it down to the two spots where the Andamans YouTube vid might have been shot. It's sixty kilometres from Port Blair and I don't know if the boys can travel that far but I decide to give it a crack. I've made up my mind that this is my swan song, my last attempt at getting somewhere to myself. There's a solid swell due and it's forecast to last for five days.

I'm just about to fuck off when they arrive, chugging around the breakwater, and I see straightaway that his boat's not going to cut it. It's run-down and slow as shit. They see me and smile and wave, and I help them tie up on the dock.

"Gidday mate!" calls the boy. He's grinning, delighted with himself.

"Gidday mate," I say back, and he smiles even more.

When they're up on the dock I introduce myself. The boy's Tala and his dad's Firoz. I tell them I want to visit Little Andaman to surf, and Firoz nods and thinks about it. His boy's jabbering at him but Firoz is taking no notice.

"Not this boat," I say, pointing to their fishing tub.

"Not this, not this," says Firoz. "I have boat."

They take me to see it. It's a long-tail boat of about twenty five feet, with a canopy covering the central part of the deck. I've seen how fast they can go and if there's not much wind I reckon we should be right.

"Yours?" I ask.

He nods in an unconvincing way but it doesn't much matter.

"How long to get to Little Andaman?"

Firoz holds up four fingers.

"How much?"

He makes a point of thinking about this for a while.

"One hundred twenty US dollars for day," he says hopefully, and he's trying to play it cool but I see the flash in his eyes when I accept.

"Four days. Four eighty," I say, and he nods enthusiastically. Tala's eyes bulge out of his head.

"Here. Tomorrow morning. 6am," I say.

He nods.

"No Tala. Just you." I don't want to feel responsible for the boy.

"Yes. No Tala," he agrees.

The next morning they're both there when I arrive, sheepishly grinning at me.

"Tala come now," says Firoz.

I say nothing. I had a feeling it would happen anyway.

Tala is quivering with excitement, and he takes my board bag off me and immediately rams it into the side of the boat. His father kicks out at him, yelling, but I can tell the show is for my benefit only. Tala skips away out of reach, laughing.

It takes an hour to get underway because something's wrong with the engine. Firoz pulls pieces off it and lays them out on the seats and just when I think it's all over he crows and holds up the offending engine part. It's a short length of pipe which he sucks and blows on, and then forcefully spits a mouthful of petrol through. He lights up a bidi immediately afterwards and puffs happily away on it as he holds the pipe up to the light. He's satisfied with his work and fifteen minutes later we're chugging out of the harbour entrance.

Firoz winds it up on the open sea and it's a loud, smoky old bastard of an engine but we're moving fast and the sea is glossy and smooth.

I pull my old Hammo out of the board bag and sure enough Tala has dinged the rail so I plug it with Solarez while the kid watches. He's so into it that I have to keep pushing him away so I can see what I'm doing. I ditched the new Hammo back on Simeulue – I just left it in the rack – so now I'm just down to this board and my old 6'9" gun.

Four hours later we're working our way along the coast of a large island off to our right, and Firoz nods when I ask if it's Little Andaman. I ask him to go closer and he turns towards the coast a little bit but seems reluctant to alter his course too much. When a breakwater comes into view I realise that we've passed one of the spots I wanted to check out and ask him to go back but he shakes his head and points at the engine and then at the breakwater. I don't argue – there's only a small discernible swell so there'll be no surfing today anyway.

As soon as we dock at Little Andaman, Firoz starts pulling the engine apart again and tells me tomorrow we surf so I walk into town to see if I can find somewhere to stay. Firoz and Tala are going to sleep on the boat but it's windless and stifling and I can't face it.

I ask a few locals but they just stare at me in silence so I keep going. I've got used to the Indo kids chattering and running alongside me but it's a different vibe here. There's a restaurant and I go in and point at something on the menu and they seem surprised that I'm ordering it. I can't tell what it is when it arrives and it tastes fucking weird but I'm starving so I wolf it down and hope it doesn't give me the shits.

I mimed sleeping to the restaurant owner and he pointed down the street so I keep going and find what looks to be the only hotel in town. It's a run-down guest house and there's no one behind the desk but there's a fan in the corner so I sit in front of it and wait. Turns out it's the only fan in the place and they won't let me take it to my room so I sweat like a dog and hardly sleep all night.

The next morning I'm up at dawn and back at the jetty and in the dim light I can see the occasional puff of white at the end of the breakwater as a wave hits. We motor out of the bay and around the breakwater and we're into the swell and I can see that it's not epic but it should be on somewhere.

I get Firoz to head north to a spot not far away that I sussed out on Google Maps but it's mushing around the point and not connecting through. I can tell straightaway it's not the spot.

We turn around and motor south again for an hour, hugging the coast. There's plenty of righthanders all down the coast and I get Firoz to stop while I surf one of them, but it's not even close to what I saw in the video.

We go as far south as we can and I know there's only one last place it could be and if it's not I've been hoodwinked. I get Firoz to open it up and we charge across the bay. A northerly is blowing and as we get closer I can see a promising rooster tail of spray being hoisted from the humping back of a wave. I turn Firoz deeper into the bay so that we can get a good look at it from the side and something clicks in my brain. At a certain point I get a view of the wave and the trees on the island in the background, and I know that this is it. A charge like an electric shock runs through me. There are three-foot runners winding for two hundred metres down the reef with mechanised regularity, each wave a perfect facsimile of the one before and the one following.

Tala and Firoz watch with interest as I smear sunscreen on my face and wax my board. I pull on a rashie and dive overboard. It's so good to be in the water that I grin like an idiot all the way to the take-off.

The first wave I catch I just cruise, looking all around me, taking it in. The reef passing beneath me is a treasure chest of jewels strewn across the sea floor. The water is blood warm and the breeze is like silk. I can hear Tala hooting from the boat. The wave is ridiculously uniform, and I look back into its eye as it playfully chases after me. Already I'm thinking about tomorrow, when the swell kicks in earnest, but for now I'm blissfully happy.

I surf for four hours, and gradually it builds until five footers are showing up on a regular basis. I get covered up on nearly every wave. When I get back to the boat, I'm almost too tired to pull myself in, and I lie on the floor for a moment smiling up at Firoz and Tala, who's looking at me like I'm some sort of deity. I wish I'd brought the creased Hammo with me and given it to him; the boy was hooked.

We head back to the jetty and I walk into town and order another suspect meal from the restaurant before collapsing into bed, happier than I've been in months. I'm excited for tomorrow, but I'm so rooted that I sleep like a baby.

The next day's a different kettle of fish. As soon as we get out of the bay we're into solid groundswell, broad and powerful lumps of ocean travelling northwards with the speed and gravity of ocean liners. Firoz and Tala are quiet on the way to the point, and I'm nervous as fuck. I eat nuts and prunes and drink water and make sure the fins are tight in my gun. I re-tie my leggie. The Hammo won't be required today.

The point is heaving. The first wave I see puts my heart in my mouth. It breaks with the crack and rumble of a thunderstorm; its gaping barrel a treacherous black cave. The breeze today is fresher, and towering cumulonimbus clouds block out the sun. I've been looking up at them, hanging in the sky like shadowy portents, like they're so heavy they could collapse and fall.

The waves are eight to ten foot, and beyond my capability; I have no doubt of that. I've surfed bigger, but only over a sand bottom and in water too murky to see it, not above antlers of coral in shallow, gin-clear water. The intimidation factor is off-the-scale, and I just sit on my board in the channel for a while, watching it. I get more nervous with every wave that passes, like they're notches on a cog, each one gradually tightening a coiled spring.

There's a whistle from the boat. Tala's waiting for the show to start, impatiently flicking his hand to encourage me to get into it. I realise it's as good a motivation as any: I didn't come this far to watch.

I paddle to the take-off zone. My fear tells me to shoulder hop, but my head tells me I'm more likely to go over the falls if I do. I force myself deeper, and wait for a set and it's not long until it looms.

I hear Tala screaming from the boat as I paddle into the first wave, and it heaves beneath me like a snorting rhino and I pull back. The view over the edge is horrific; if anything it seems shallower than yesterday. The power of it as it breaks forces jets of water through the back of the wave and they froth and spritz and rain down on me.

The second wave's a carbon copy and I stroke hard but pull back again. The drop's the most appalling thing I've ever seen.

"Faarrk!" I scream, disgusted with myself, turning back to the ocean.

There's yet another wave, just as perfect, just as daunting. This time I'm driven by a sort of madness; a self-loathing. I don't give a shit. I paddle into it with everything I've got and I'm into it early and on my feet. I'm stiff with fear, but I make the drop and bottom turn and I'm slung out onto the face, my board chattering with speed. I straight-line it, gun it, outrunning the tube, too freaked out to do anything but set my line and look around me in disbelief. It's beyond perfect; it's like no other wave I've ever surfed. There's a power thrumming beneath my board that I've never felt before.

I give a guttural scream of delight as I pull off the wave and look back to the boat. I see Tala, but to my surprise he's not looking at me; he's looking out to sea. There's a final wave in the set but when it clears I see what he's looking at. Brian's schooner is creaming around the point, and I can already see the boys waxing their boards and pulling on rashies.

Chapter 12

We're half-way back to Port Blair when I feel the heat rising on my forehead and the rumble in my guts. I've said barely two words to Firoz, and I know he's worried that he's going to miss out on a day's pay. He and Tala wanted to know why I didn't surf with the other guys, why I simply paddled back to the boat and told Firoz to pull up the anchor and start the engine.

"You want surf wave alone?" he asked, and I simply nodded and said nothing.

By the time we get back to Port Blair I've vomited three times and had to jump over the side twice to take a shit. Firoz told me just to hang my arse over the side, but I can't handle shitting and being watched by the kid. I'm hot one minute and cold the next, and I just want to get back to the hotel.

I say goodbye to Firoz and Tala and start walking to the road to hail a tuk-tuk. I feel like I'm going to shit myself and I clench my arse cheeks and pray.

"Jimmy?"

I turn and it's Firoz, and he looks all around and then comes close and talks in a whisper. It's like a bad spy movie and I almost laugh out loud. He says he knows another spot where the waves break like they were today, but it's not allowed; it's forbidden to go there.

"I bring you, but you mustn't say anyone," he says, staring at me intently.

"Nicobar?" I ask.

Firoz nods. "The government not allow people to go there. Have to be very careful. I know how," he says, tapping his chest.

"When?" I ask. The sweat is pouring off my head.

"Tomorrow? Next day? I ready when you are."

I consider it for less than a second.

"No Tala this time," I say.

"No Tala," he agrees.

I have to take a dump badly and I make for a gap between two wharf buildings where my arse basically explodes. I can see two dock workers peering at me but at this point I don't give a fuck.

It's two days before I'm able to get back to the wharf. I'm still as weak as a kitten and about five kilos lighter but I feel OK and I know I'm past the worst of it. Trouble is I can't find Firoz. I sit there for a couple of hours but he's a no-show so I wander off to find some lunch. Every bite I take I'm wondering if I'll see it again in liquid form.

When I get back to the wharf Firoz is there with Tala. They're unloading their catch, but it looks like they caught next to nothing.

"Any luck?" I say, and they look up and smile at me like I'm their long-lost relative. I point at their basket and ask again if the fishing was any good but Firoz says the fishing is always bad these days.

"We thought you gone home Australia," he says, and both he and Tala laugh when I shake my head and point at my arse.

I make a plan to meet Firoz at 5am the next day. The swell forecast for the next few days is two-and-a-half to three metres at sixteen seconds, and the wind is light and from the north. I just hope Firoz knows what he's talking about.

I half expect to see Tala in the morning but it's only Firoz. He's already tinkering around in the motor with the light from his phone, but it starts first go and we're off into the oily black sea. Fifteen minutes out and it's completely dark but for the stars but Firoz seems to know where he's going, whistling tunelessly over the noise of the motor.

"How long?" I ask him.

"One hour," he replies, and I'm surprised because the Nicobars are further south than Little Andaman. I was expecting five hours. I get the creeping sense that this is going to be a wild goose chase.

As it gets light I can see islands to the left and the right but as they drop away the boat starts to rise and fall over the swell. It's small, but the further away from the islands we get the more it builds until we're speeding over some decent lumps.

I notice a difference in Firoz. He's no longer whistling, and he's scanning the horizon constantly, searching for other boats. He motions for me to come back to him in the stern.

"We not allowed here," he says, pointing ahead of us. "Nicobar."

I nod, but I'm confused.

In the distance is a low smudge of land.

"Surf there," he says. "North Sentinel Island."

Something clicks and whirrs in my memory. I've heard of the place. I remember it was in the news when some missionary tried to go there to bring god to the locals and they murdered him there and then on the beach and the Indian government wouldn't even recover the body. There was a flurry of stories about it, and I remember finding a YouTube clip of some old footage taken from a boat where you could see the natives on the beach, jumping around and firing arrows at the boat. It looked mental as fuck.

"How am I going to surf there? They'll kill me!" I say to Firoz.

He shakes his head and holds out his hand, palm up. He prods it at either end with his finger.

"Island here, surf here," he says. "Safe."

"They've got bows and arrows," I say.

He shakes his head again.

"Too far," he says.

"Have they got boats? Canoes?" I can't believe I'm discussing this.

"Yes, canoe, but no engine," says Firoz, patting the growling beast behind him. "Sometimes they chase us if we fish there. They too slow."

A cold fear creeps up my spine. I feel like I'm going to shit myself again. Last night I spent half an hour talking to Jess and we pretty much made up properly and I found myself looking forward to getting home to see her. She'd freak if she knew what I was doing now.

As we plough on in the growing light I watch as the island goes from a hazy dark strip to densely forested land. Firoz makes for the southern tip of the island, keeping his distance. He's on high alert, ready to turn the boat around at any moment. The swells are now uniform, corduroy lines, and I can see whitewater on the reefs all around the island, broken only by a number of promising looking reef passes. There isn't a breath of wind.

When we get close enough I scan the beach through an old pair of binoculars Firoz hands me, but there's nothing but white sand leading up to dense jungle. There's no sign of people; no huts, no canoes.

I'm so busy looking at the island that I don't even notice that we've come in sight of the wave until Firoz whistles at me and points. I look along the coast and I see it immediately. It's a lefthander, and as I watch a six-foot wave caps on the outside, a gutless layer of whitewater sliding down its face. My heart sinks. But almost immediately the wave begins to rear and it's as though the whitewater is levered up from the face and flung towards shore. Suddenly I'm looking into the eye of a gaping cavern. Chandeliers of foam drop with the lip like whites in a spin dryer. It roars across the reef and turns itself inside out with a furious puff. I think that must be it, but the wave continues to grind, and then, unbelievably, remoulds itself into an exquisite crystalline pipe, barrelling across the reef for another hundred metres. It spits again, spray huffing out over the channel.

Three hundred metres away, on the opposite side of the pass, a right-hander is doing almost exactly the same thing.

It's the best set-up I've ever seen, no question. I look at Firoz and he's smiling at me and nodding with pride, like he's the best surf boat captain the world has ever known. And he might just be. I hoot and clap him on the back and he pulls out his bidi and rewards me with a toothless grin.

We motor into the centre of the pass and Firoz drops the anchor. I see he only puts a couple of loops over the cleat, and he sits beside it, ready to go quickly.

I alternate between watching the waves and scanning the shoreline with the binoculars. It's about four hundred metres to the beach from where the wave ends. There isn't a soul to be seen.

Finally, I make up my mind. I'm nervous as fuck as I throw the Hammo overboard and dive after it. Firoz is on the binoculars, and he says he'll whistle if he sees anything. He'll up-anchor and meet me halfway to the waves, he says.

"Come very fast to me," he says.

"Don't worry about that," I reply.

I choose the left. The roll-in is just too good. Like two dancers coming together, I make it to the take-off spot just as a wave arrives. It actually breaks outside me a bit, but I catch the foam and ride out of it on my guts and lazily get to my feet. I weave a little, getting my groove on. There's all the time in the world.

I fade a little as the wave starts to rear, then bottom turn and check into one of the sweetest barrels of my life.

Light sparkles and refracts and turns my cave into a crystal palace. I stand straight and feel the top of the tube skim my head. The chandeliers threaten to close the door but I'm flying now and I simply duck a little to get under them. I'm in there for a good six seconds before skimming out onto the face with blinding speed. I rise and rise up the face, and then lay into a cutty. I think I can actually hear my fins slicing through the water. I bounce off the foam and work the face as vertically as I can. I almost blow my last turn because the wave is racing off again, and I just sneak under the lip and then I'm in the barrel again. I'm deep and speeding for all I'm worth but I get clipped before I can make it out.

I come up hooting, but then remember where I am and immediately look towards shore. There's nobody. Firoz gives me a thumbs up as I pass. I'm in heaven.

The morning passes in a kind of dream. I'm so dialled in to the wave that I feel like I've been surfing here all my life. I can barely paddle, my arms are that sore, but I can't bring myself not to get one more, and one more after that.

Firoz and I are so busy scanning the shore or looking for the next wave that neither of us notices the outrigger canoe that comes around the coast from the east. I paddle over a perfect set, too exhausted to turn and catch one, and there it is, coming straight for me. There are three people aboard. The sight puts the heart across me, adrenaline lights up my body. I strike out for the boat in a thrashing frenzy and I'm screaming out to Firoz but he can't hear me over the surf. I see him peering at the shore through his binoculars. I know they'll catch me easily and I glance back, and I almost cry with relief when I see that it's only kids. I stop paddling and turn around to have a good look. They do the same to me. They're the darkest-skinned people I've ever seen, and all three are completely naked. The girl stands up in the boat holding her paddle, and I can see she's about twelve. There's a younger boy of about eight or nine, and a younger one again

– another little boy about five. I wave to them, but they simply stare at me in silence. I realise that I'm probably the first white man they've ever seen.

When I catch sight of the dark swells rising beyond them, I know already that it's too late. I shout at the kids and point and wave my arms. They just stare back at me. It's only when the first wave starts to break that the girl looks seaward. A look of panic crosses her face and she sits down immediately, thrusting her paddle into the water and shouting a command at her brother. They paddle as fast as they can, but they're well inside and the wave catches them in the worst possible place, mowing them down in an explosion of whitewater. I see the canoe shoot out before the wave, upside down, its occupants gone. I turn and paddle towards them for all I'm worth.

By the time I've made it halfway they've been hit by two more waves. Each time I see the heads of the older two kids pop up, but the young boy is nowhere to be seen. I hear the girl screaming in fear as each wave bears down upon her. I keep going, puffing hard and aiming roughly at where I think the boy might be.

I'm in the white water when I hear Firoz's whistle. I ignore it, and finding myself in shallow water, I stand up on the coral and scan the foam for the boy. The girl is standing too, screaming and crying. I see the older lad down the reef a bit, and I can see he's safe and clambering up onto the coral.

Suddenly the girl rushes forward, shouting. She bends and pulls the boy out of the water. His body's limp, his head rag-dolling to one side, mouth gaping open. I go to her, the coral slicing my feet, but there's so much adrenaline in my veins that I'm oblivious to the pain.

We're in knee-deep water by the time I reach them, and the girl's holding his face up, crying and yelling to him. She shakes him, and his head wobbles grotesquely like one of those figurines on the dashboard of a car.

I grab him from her and she tries to hold on to him, but I rip him away and lay him on his back on my surfboard. I think she's going to launch herself at me and I brace myself but she simply stands behind me and howls, a chilling, dreadful wail.

The boy looks long gone, but I reach into his mouth and feel for his tongue. It's retracted, settled in the back of his throat, and I hook my finger around it and pull it forward and press it down into place. We get smacked by whitewater and I have to do it all again. Then I pinch his nose, tilt his head back, clamp my mouth around his and blow. I see his chest rise and fall.

Firoz's whistle comes again, long and urgent. I glance towards the shore and I can see them – five or six men, dragging outriggers down the beach at a sprint. They slingshot them into the water and leap in, their paddles flashing like swords.

I give the boy another breath and another, but there's no response.

By now the older lad has made it across the reef to us and he watches in shocked silence as I do CPR on the boy. But it's difficult on the surfboard and the boy slides around on it and I can't get enough compression. I go down on my knees and try to ignore the pain of it as I pull the board and boy on to my thighs and keep going. I grab the other side of the board with one hand and find I can give him a decent compression with the other. I pound on the boy's chest as fast and as hard as I can, forgetting whatever the fuck I learned in the first aid course I took years ago.

The older lad thinks I'm hurting the boy and comes at me, but I push him away and he staggers and falls on the coral and I keep going, over and over, stopping only to give the boy a quick breath.

A third whistle from Firoz rises over the sound of the surf and my own panicked gasps and I look up at him. He's in the channel, as close as he dares come, so close I can see the look of desperation on his face. He waves his arms at me wildly and turns the boat in circles.

I glance back towards shore and the canoes are halfway across the lagoon and coming fast. There's a man standing in the bow of each, and it's hard to see but I think they're holding bows and aiming them in my direction.

I keep going on the boy, furiously pumping his chest. It's awful watching him slide around on the top of my board, so limp and lifeless. I stop and go to breathe into his mouth again, but the boy coughs, and water bubbles up out of his mouth like a spring. I turn his head to the side and it pours out, then I sit him up and push him forward and he vomits. I can't believe how much water comes out and it's mixed with the yellow bile of his stomach.

I check for a pulse and I think I can feel something fluttering under my fingertips, but it's hard to tell with the surf and the howling girl and my own heart beating like a drum.

I gather him in my arms and bring his face up to mine and I think I can feel his breath and then I'm sure of it. He starts to wriggle, and in a moment I'll never forget as long as I live, he opens his eyes. They take a second to focus but then he's looking up into my face as if nothing had happened, like a child waking up in the morning. In that moment I get a rush of emotion so strong it pulses through me like a drug. I can't believe that I've saved his life.

The canoes are a hundred metres away. In each there's a man paddling on either side and one standing on the bow. They've split; one of them is coming for us, and the other is heading up the middle of the channel. When I turn to look for Firoz I already know what I'm going to see. He's two hundred metres away, motoring out towards the open ocean. He's looking back at me, shaking his head and throwing up his arms in despair. The man on the bow of the canoe chasing him looses an arrow at him, but Firoz is too far away and it falls harmlessly into the sea.

I stagger to my feet, still holding the boy in my arms. He's lying still, not moving at all, looking up into my face.

I turn to watch the canoe as they paddle the last fifty metres to the reef. My heart is pounding; I can feel it pulsing in my ears.

I'm sick with fear, but also I feel a deep exhaustion, a dizzying lethargy that doesn't allow me to do anything but stand there, swaying slightly, clutching the child.

The men are naked aside from a thick woven belt around their waists and a golden necklace. Their skin is glossy with sea spray and sweat; their muscles gleam and ripple. The one up front has his bow drawn back to his cheek and he's aiming it directly at me, and I know the only reason he hasn't fired yet is because of the boy in my arms.

He barks orders at the paddlers and they bring the canoe side-on to the fringe of the reef, then two of them leap out and run across the coral towards us like it's nothing more than a grassy field. The bowman yells to the older kids and they call back and immediately move towards the men. The girl is speaking rapidly, a high-pitched torrent of words, anguished and frightened.

The man strides past her and she turns, still talking to him, but he ignores her and I can see murder in his eyes as he reaches me and rips the child from my arms. He looks briefly at the boy and then hands him to the girl. The second man has reached me, and he's still holding his paddle in his hand. I hear the girl scream in protest, but he raises it over his head and I don't even lift my arms up to protect myself as he delivers the blow. Then I'm back in the water, lying face-down in the shallows. There's a hum in the back of my skull. My eyes are open, and I can see colours, smudged watercolours of aquamarine and emerald and cerise. I can hear the crackling sounds of the creatures of the reef, and the hush of the surf.

He must have hit me again because that's the last thing I remember.

PART TWO

Chapter 13

The days following the rescue are a nightmarish haze. I sleep much of the day in a torpor so deep it's like I've been drugged, and then at nights I lie half-conscious in a fevered state, sweating and shivering, my body cramping viciously in the dark. I know sometimes that I shout out in my sleep, and I'm jerking and twitching all the time, endlessly falling in my dreams.

Sometimes I think I feel hands on me. Something soft and cool passes over my forehead. Water is poured over my body. I'm dragged across the floor every now and then.

The light is dim all the time during the day, and in a moment of lucidity I realise that I must be deep in the jungle but I can't drag myself to the door of the hut I'm in to look out. Through the opening I can see only trees, and sometimes I wake thinking I've seen the wide-eyed stares of kids watching me. But then the fever hits and I'm gone again, back into the awful darkness.

Finally I pass through some sort of threshold. Bit by bit things start to make sense; I become more aware. The sounds of the village start to penetrate my haze, coming to me through the walls. It's all but silent during the heat of the day, but towards the afternoon and evening I hear talking and children playing. I hear arguments, the high-pitched protest of women and the guttural, machine-gun barks of men. I hear a proper scrap one evening, I'm sure of it; the thud and slap of skin on skin, the grunts of effort. But there are no raised voices, no excited chatter that normally accompanies a fight.

Someone's given me water, a hollow length of a stalk, like a segment of bamboo, but soft and bound at the base with a fibrous twine. I see it leaning against the wall by my head, but I don't know what it is, and when I tilt it to look inside I pour it over myself. I lie there, sucking what I can off my arms and hands, gasping like a goldfish, until I pass out again. When I wake a few hours later, it's back against the wall, refilled. There's also a piece of bark with something on it, and I chew it slowly, realising as the taste is released that it's dried fish. I have to take small sips of water between each bite because I can't muster a drop of saliva.

I don't know how long this goes on for – maybe a couple of days, but finally I feel better and then I'm driven out of the hut because I need to take a shit. I know that biologically it's good news, but my heart's fucking pounding when I muster the courage to stick my head out of the door.

It must be sometime around the middle of the day because there's no one around and it's stinking hot. There's nothing but the hum of insects as I creep silently behind my hut and drop my boardies, and my thighs shake like mad when I squat. It runs out of me like a tap, and for a moment I'm freaking that I've got cholera or something else, but then I get a solid bit at the end and it calms me down. I wonder have I been shitting myself in the hut the whole time.

I wipe my arse with a handful of leaves and kick forest litter over my pathetic effort.

When I was squatting, I could see underneath my hut. There's twenty or so huts built in a circle around a huge tree in the centre, whose canopy shades the whole place. The earth has been trodden flat all around it. It's a storybook headquarters, as though dreamed up by a bunch of kids.

There isn't a soul in the village, and I have no plan, but my instinct is overwhelming and irresistible. I turn and walk away from the village into the jungle. I move as quietly as I can but I'm snapping twigs and rustling past foliage and my heart's in my mouth. I have the awful premonition of an arrow buried deep between my shoulder blades but I don't look back. The jungle's almost impenetrable and it's hard going. My knees and feet are stiff from the reef cuts, but it dawns on me that there's no infection there, and I realise that someone must have been taking care of them when I was in the hut or they'd be pus-ridden sores by now. The side of my head also has a pulpy wound on it; I brush my hand over it and it comes away covered in a greenish slime.

I'm weak as fuck and soon I have to stop and hang onto a branch because I'm so dizzy I might fall over otherwise. I stand, swaying slightly, waiting for my balance to return. The only sound I can hear is the whine of the mozzies congregating around my legs. I watch them for a while; they don't land on me but keep their distance as though I've rubbed on repellant.

When I look up again there's a Sentinelese woman just five metres away, standing there as still as a rock. I didn't even hear her approach. She doesn't move a muscle or say anything, but simply stares at me, wide-eyed. There's a knife in a sheath on her waistband, but she doesn't draw it.

She's small, less than five feet tall. She's maybe twenty or twenty five years old. She's completely naked, an ebony statue against the lush green backdrop of the jungle. Along with her waistband, she wears a hoop necklace that looks like it's made from steel, and a golden headband. Her hair is short and tight to her scalp, shaved high up her forehead.

She looks just as afraid as I am; urgency and fear flashes in her eyes. She points back at the village and I know it's an instruction:

turn around, go back. It occurs to me that maybe it's not me she's afraid of, but the men of the village and what they'll do if they discover that I'm gone. For a second I consider pushing past her, but it dawns upon me how unprepared and vulnerable I am. I'm weak as hell. I'm hungry. I have only a pair of boardies to my name. I'm on an island a long way from anywhere.

The woman has decided that I'm not a threat; I'm still hanging onto the tree to stay upright. She walks towards me, taking quick, nimble steps through the tangle of the jungle. She's like a bird. She comes right up to me, puts her hand on my chest and pushes me, turning me back towards the village. I do what I'm bid, and I stumble back. She pushes me from time to time, and I realise she's keeping me on track; I keep veering away from the path without realising it.

We get back to the village and there's still no one around. She pushes me towards the hut and I climb back up into it. I'm barely able to heave myself up and through the entrance, and when I get inside I collapse heavily on to the floor. I'm sweating like a dog and now that the adrenaline has abandoned me, I'm shot.

The woman is suddenly beside me, rolling me on to my back. She holds the reed and pours water into my mouth. She goes out again and comes back with more water and washes the dirt and sticks from my feet, examining my cuts closely. They sting like fuck. She has a small bowl filled with a bright green paste which she smears over the soles of my feet. Some of the cuts must have reopened, and I gasp, but she ignores me. She scoops the rest of the paste from the bowl and rubs it over the cuts on my knees.

I try to lie quietly while she tends to me. Up close, I notice the notches cut into her earlobes, the scars on her hands. Her fingers are strong, her arms and neck lean and muscular. This close I can see that her necklace really is made from steel; I can see the ripples and dents in it where it has been hammered into shape. I wonder where she got it.

There's no hint of self-consciousness about her nakedness in front of me; she moves freely. She doesn't look at my face once.

She disappears and comes back with a spiral shell in her hands. She tips it and a yellow, thick oil pours out on to my legs. She rubs it all over them, then more on my arms. My nostrils fill with a strong vegetable odour and it occurs to me that it's the insect repellant. She gets me to turn over and rubs it on my back. Then she's gone.

I sleep the rest of that day and all night. The village rises at first light, and I'm woken by kids giggling outside the hut. A woman snaps at them and they run away. I sit up. There's no fog in my head, no sweat on my brow. The fire in my limbs has gone. Beside me are two full tubes of water and more dried fish. I finish all of them. I feel better, but there's still a deep exhaustion in my body.

I badly need to piss and consider doing it into the water tube, but I know that what I'm storing will overflow it and besides, I don't know what I'll do with it afterwards. I have to go out. I feel my fear build again. It thickens my thoughts, sucks the saliva from my mouth. Before I was too sick to be afraid; now that I'm almost well it rises like a tide, quickening my heart. I try to take some deep breaths to calm down.

I lower myself as silently as I can out of the opening of the hut. I don't even look in the direction of the clearing, but walk as quietly as I can around the back of my hut. I piss against a tree trunk so that the urine flows down it quietly. I'm half expecting to be clubbed over the back of the head at any moment, and I'm hunched over in preparation, but I finish my piss and get my boardies back up. I hear a sound behind me and when I turn there's a bunch of kids standing there and I know the time has come. I can see that the older kids are frightened by me and the babies stare with a naked fascination.

Finally one of them can't take it anymore and runs screaming into the village. I don't move a muscle; I don't want to get any closer to the kids and I know I won't make it any further than fifty metres into the jungle.

I don't have to wait long. Men come streaming around the huts. Some of them have their bows, but the closest one holds a deadly looking stone adze and he raises it above his head as he reaches me. I know this could be it, but I can't just drop my head and accept the blow, so I go for him. He yells at me, and thinks I'm going to stop, but I just run right into him, rugby-tackling him as hard as I can. He folds in half. The adze hits me in the back, and I know it's going to hurt like fuck later, but I'm oblivious to the pain as I smash into him. He's probably only fifty kilos, and I lift him off his feet and drive him back a few metres before poleaxing him into the ground. The adze clatters away. We scrap like wild animals on the dirt and he's strong as fuck, and it's only luck that I smash the back of my head up into his jaw.

There's a hard kick to my ribs as the next man arrives, but I'm up and turning towards him, and I use my momentum to smack him a good one in the face and he goes down too. Then there are men all around me, and I'm expecting a knife or an arrow in the back any second but there's a command from one of them and they all hold off, surrounding me with their bows and knives ready. The guy I tackled looks at me with a murderous rage as he wheezes to his feet and collects his adze.

I'm like a cornered animal, wild-eyed and breathing in ragged gasps, and it's the only sound in the silent jungle. The women and children of the tribe have crept up behind the men.

The Sentinelese who gave the order to stop walks up to me and I'm ready to have a go at him too, but he simply stares at me. There's no anger in his features, no urgency in his movements. He calmly looks me over.

I'm as scared as I've ever been but I force myself to return his gaze, to emulate his self-assuredness. My heart feels like it's going to beat out of my chest.

I assume he's the chief. He's small but wiry and strong, the muscles in his arms like knotted ship ropes. I reckon he's about thirty five, or maybe a little older. He wears nothing but a waistband, into which is tucked a flat stone club.

He speaks to me, and his language is like nothing I've ever heard, a staccato rattle of consonants and clicks.

I shake my head, tell him that I don't understand; that I don't speak his language. I speak for long enough for him to realise he doesn't speak mine, and I see his eyes widen as he listens to the bizarre sounds I'm making.

I can see the chief thinking, considering everything about me. He comes closer and looks not into my eyes but at them. He moves from side to side, inspecting them like a doctor looking for cataracts. He then moves on to my hair, but he doesn't touch it. He seems intrigued by the hair on my arms and chest.

Pointing at my hands, he gestures for me to lift them up and I show him my palms. He compares them to his. A ripple of conversation goes around the men and some of the children try to push forward to see but they're held back by the women.

The man I tackled is still fuming. Blood from where I split his lip with the back of my head is spread over his teeth, and it dribbles on to his feet as he starts to speak to the chief, angry and insistent. Without a word the chief steps to him, his stone cudgel suddenly flashing in his hand. He drives it into the man's throat and the guy makes a strangled gasp and crumples on to the ground. He's fighting for breath, his eyes bulging. He must have bitten his tongue, and a fresh crimson ooze pours out of his mouth.

Calmly the chief returns his attention back to me, resuming his impassive inspection, but his sudden violence has freaked me out so badly that I can't help myself; I turn and run. I burst through two of the men and head for the jungle and behind me I hear the chief's command. I know this is it but I keep running, weaving between trees and leaping over fallen logs. I trip and crash to the ground and get up again, staggering and smashing my way through the undergrowth, barbed vines tearing at my legs.

I run until I can't run anymore. I glance behind me now and again but I don't see anyone. But now I'm swaying on my feet like a punch-drunk boxer and there's no way I can protect myself again. A child could knock me over.

When I turn and take a good look back into the jungle I see the chief coming after me, unhurriedly stepping through the undergrowth. I think about hiding, throwing myself under a log or something, but I know he could find me with his eyes closed so I wait for him. I look around for a decent weapon and choose a half-rotten branch, but I've seen what he can do with his club and I know I don't stand a chance.

But when the chief reaches me he simply points back towards the village. His stone club is tucked into the back of his waistband and he doesn't reach for it, even though he sees the branch in my hand. In the silence he simply stares at me, confidently waiting for me to come to the decision to do what he says. When I drop the branch he says something to me and sets off, knowing I'll follow him. Which I do. I'm close enough behind him that I could rip his stone club from his waistband and whack him over the head with it, but he doesn't turn around even once.

When we get back to the village they're all waiting for us. There's not a shred of surprise on any of their faces. I can tell the one whose lip I split is still mad as fuck, so I don't look at him. But it's hard not to stare; it's like a scene from National Geographic and by incremental degrees it dawns on me just what I've got myself into. There are probably fifty adults and a dozen kids in the group, and they're watching me closely as I stumble into the ring of huts.

One of the kids sneaks out for a better look and I recognise him; it's the boy I saved. He's as good as new as far as I can tell. When the chief walks into the village, the boy runs straight to him and the chief wraps an arm around him and now I know why I'm not dead.

I stand there while they deliberate. The kids are all glued to me, but the adults don't look my way at all, even though I know they're figuring out what to do with me. The fella with the bloody mouth is itching to say something, I can tell; he quietly seethes around the outside of the group. He stares at me constantly, a filthy look in his eyes.

They're having a decent fucking discussion, that's for sure. It's an animated, rapid-fire sound, their language, but delivered with little facial expression. Both men and women speak, and they're listened to with equal gravity. The woman who's been tending my cuts, who turned me back to the village, steps forward and speaks for a long time. The boy I saved has noodled himself in, and stands against her, clinging to her leg, listening.

As it goes on I'm filled with a deepening dread; I can sense there's a serious case being made for my death. The men in particular are insistent, forceful, and I can see the chief nodding slightly as they speak. Finally, he finishes the meeting with a raised hand, and they all turn to me. A dagger of fear probes my insides. I begin to hyperventilate.

The chief walks to me in the silence. He's watching my face; sensing my terror. There's complete silence in the clearing, save for one of the children who hiccups occasionally. It strikes me as a bizarre soundtrack to the last moments of my life. No one takes any notice. They're thrilled, transfixed by whatever the fuck is about to happen.

I rise to the balls of my feet. Some deluded, defiant impulse sears through me and I decide I'll have a crack at the first one to come at me.

The chief opens his mouth to say something, but he's beaten to it by the woman who's been nursing me. She comes forward, speaking rapidly. She turns, points to the girl who's hiccupping, then falls silent.

The chief considers. He barks an order to the girl, who comes forward. She's perhaps ten or twelve years old.

The chief gently guides her in front of me. Gone is any curiosity that she might have had at a safe distance, now replaced with an obvious terror. Her eyes are like those of a wounded animal as the hunter approaches to finish it off. I know I'm losing it because all I can think of is that now I know for sure that the old wives' cure of giving someone a fright to cure hiccups is a pile of shit because she's still going like mad. I stupidly wonder if their word for hiccup is hiccup. I look instead at the chief.

He points at the girl and speaks. I have no idea what he wants. The girl's hiccups punctuate the silence, splitting it into awful moments, the countdown to something strange and probably fatal. I'm so frightened that I can't concentrate, I can't decipher him. I shake my head; tell him I no can understand. It makes no difference whether I speak like an upper-class toff or in my stupid pidgin; he isn't going to understand that I don't understand. He's just going to kill me.

He tries again, and this time he points at the girl's throat and mimics her hiccups. "Hiccups," I say, nodding. Hiccups. My brain is fizzing with fear. He stares at me. He will not try to make himself understood again, I realise; this is my last chance.

Suddenly, I know what he wants me to do: cure the girl. "Right, yes," I half shout. I'm manic as I hold up a finger, like a magician, like a circus clown. "Wait," I tell him.

I look at the woman, and desperately I mime drinking water. I point at her, pretend I'm holding the drinking tube, tip it to my mouth. I almost cry with relief when I see the recognition register in her eyes.

She disappears and comes back with a full tube of water which she hands to me, but I say no, she must hold it. The chief watches with interest.

I hold a finger up to the girl, who's breathing rapidly now, hyperventilating with terror. I make a horizontal circle with my finger to tell her to turn around and face the people, but it does no more good than if I'd said it to her, so I have to gently take her by the shoulders and spin her around. She flinches fiercely when I touch her and shrinks away, but the chief grunts something and she forces herself to be still.

I beckon the woman forward. I point to the water tube, and then to the girl, and the woman brings it to the girl's lips, but I hold up my hand and say, "wait, wait." She understands.

The girl jerks again when I put my thumbs in her ears but doesn't move away. I can feel her shaking. With my forefingers I block her nostrils. She hiccups again, a spasming tic that makes her shoulders jump.

I look at the woman and give an exaggerated nod. She raises the tube to the girl's lips, and I nod furiously. The girl begins to drink. She hiccups mid-drink but keeps going. The trick is to drink for as long as possible but there's no way I can figure to tell the woman that.

But somehow that's exactly what she does. The girl drinks and drinks, and when she wants to stop the woman says something to her and she drinks some more, almost finishing the tube.

The woman steps back from the girl and I remove my fingers and thumbs. Like a scene from a pantomime, the entire village stares expectantly at the girl, waiting and watching. Five seconds go by, ten, twenty. Then I know it's worked. The girl slinks away, back to the other children. She rubs her ears and nose vigorously, tainted by my touch.

The chief looks at me and bares his teeth in a cross between a smile and a grimace. I don't know which, or what it means. He says something while he's looking at me, but I can tell it's not me but the rest of the village that he's speaking to. Then he turns and walks away, and the men do the same. They take up bows and adzes and woven ropes and disappear into the jungle. One by one, the women, too, return to the business of their day. Only the children remain, waiting for my next trick, and the woman who just saved my life.

The realisation that I've just become the village doctor hits me like a hammer blow, and it causes a strange reaction. I can't stop myself from laughing out loud. I'm the world's first doctor in board shorts. I have no equipment, no medicines, no painkillers. I'm simply a miracle worker.

Suddenly I have to sit down, then to lie flat. I stretch out right there on the ground, the power in my body deserting me, replaced by a flooding relief and limbs which won't stop shaking.

Chapter 14

I spend most of the next two days sleeping or lying in the shade. I eat everything the woman brings me although I don't know what much of it is. There's raw and dried fish, and a wet, spongy flesh which I recoil from but force down because I'm demented with hunger. There are fruits, and mud-flavoured roots and tubers, uncooked and chewy. It dawns on me that the Sentinelese don't seem to use fire; nothing is cooked. One afternoon she brings me a chunk of honeycomb and I fall on it like a wild animal, sucking and slurping until my face is glazed with honey. I can tell she's amazed and disgusted at how much I can eat; she watches me stuff it into my mouth with naked fascination.

The woman's name is Imbi, and she's in sole charge of me because no one else comes near the hut. She's mostly silent and doesn't often look at my face. She comes and goes like a shadow. Twice I've been lying awake in the middle of the night when she's climbed into the hut and squatted by the entrance, listening for my breathing, checking on me. When she realised that I was awake she silently slipped away again.

She says nothing to me when she comes to check on me, but rather just gets to work checking my cuts and the gash on my head. When I try to talk to her she freezes and cocks her head to listen like a hunter straining to catch the sound of a distant animal. When I tapped my chest and told her I was Jimmy she said nothing but later I heard her saying it over and over to herself under her breath. She pronounced it 'Shimmy'. It wasn't until the next day that I convinced her to tell me her own name.

One day, when Imbi's with me, the boy I saved comes to the entrance and peers in. She turns and smiles at him and shoos him away, but I see the easy way between them and I know that what I suspected is true; the boy is her son. I ask his name and she tells me it's Baka. She says it so quietly that I know she doesn't want to tell me; she's like a child reluctantly sharing sweets. She's frightened of me even knowing his name.

My cuts are healing faster than I can credit. Almost all of them have closed over completely, and when Imbi washes away the green paste there are only mottled purple stripes across the soles of my feet and knees. I leave the hut in those two days only to piss or shit, and I try to hold on until everyone has left the village. The first day I'd just squatted down in the jungle when Imbi suddenly appeared. I could see her looking as I hurriedly clawed up my boardies, but she wasn't the least bit embarrassed. She looked at me curiously, with as much emotion as a woman choosing fruit at a supermarket. Then, she led me to where everyone goes – a long trench dug through the forest which they progressively move down, covering it over as they go.

Aside from Imbi, the Sentinelese largely ignore me. They rise each day at first light, and an hour later they're all gone from the village, employed with the business of finding food. There's no agriculture, and no planting of crops. They don't appear to eat birds or animals; everything is caught from the ocean or foraged from the ground.

One morning Imbi appears and grabs my arm, urging me out of the hut. The entire village is gathered, waiting for me, and I start to freak. I wonder if I've transgressed somehow, broken some unknown taboo with a sacrilegious act. There's total silence as I walk out into the clearing.

The chief's grimace-smile is as ambiguous as ever and the rollercoaster of fear is taking its toll on me. I find myself wildly looking around for an escape route I know doesn't exist.

He freaks the shit out of me when he says "Jimmy," but then I realise stupidly that Imbi has told him my name. I know his; Imbi pointed to him one day, tapping her chest and then pointing to him. Eda, she called him.

I try it out on him, and he smiles and nods, but he has other things on his mind.

He turns and speaks and a woman steps forward. A little girl tries to stop her by tugging at her hand, pulling her back and crying, but everyone ignores her. The woman is only slightly taller than her child. She comes forward and Eda holds her face and pulls opens her jaw. He turns to me. "Jimmy," he says again, and he stands there, waiting. The woman is whimpering.

I come forward and look into her mouth and I see immediately that one of her teeth, a molar right at the back, is infected. The gum around it is red and swollen and pus seeps around its edges. Eda looks into her mouth and jabs it with his finger, and she writhes in pain, but he holds her face firmly and laughs as she tries to pull away. "Jimmy," he says again.

Together we peer into her mouth. This close to Eda there's an animal smell to him, an earthy odour. It's the same smell that comes from Imbi, but it's more powerful off the chief.

I reach in carefully with my finger and gently give it a wiggle. It moves a bit, and pus squeezes out from the gum. She moans. I try to grab it between my thumb and forefinger, but it's difficult to get a decent grip because it's so far back, and I can tell right away that it's anchored more strongly than I can manage.

I need a tool. I look around the village, but everything's made of wood and shell and bone. But some of the men have knives in their waistbands, and I point at one of them and look back at Eda until he gives the word and the man passes it to me. It's a rough piece of steel which looks like it was sharpened on a rock. I can't think where it might have come from. Thin rope made from fibrous flax is bound around it to make a handle. The knife has a reasonable point on it, and I take it back to where the woman stands, still held firmly by Eda. A wild thought bullies its way into my head; that I could drive the knife into the chief's belly and kill him right now.

Instead, I motion for the woman to lie down, but no one understands me until I lie down myself to demonstrate. Eda says something to her. but she protests. I can imagine what she's saying – that it's all right, that it doesn't really hurt that much – but Eda is curious now and he barks at her. She lies down.

She's as wide-eyed as a spooked horse. I know she's going to thrash with the pain. I call Imbi and get her to hold down the woman's head. I have Eda hold her arms. I point at another woman and Imbi calls her over. I get her to hold the woman's jaw open.

If only Mum could see me now, I think. I take a deep breath and blow it out, like a nervous runner at the start line. I'm sure it doesn't make my patient feel any better, but it settles me a bit and I kneel down in the dirt. I see how the glossy black skin of their arms is in stark contrast to mine – hairy and freckled, and big. I feel like a giant beside them. I'm self-conscious beside the women; I'm not yet used to their nakedness. The scent is strong in our huddle, rich and loamy. I wonder how I smell to them. Bloody awful, probably.

First I have to loosen the tooth in its socket. I reach in and try to grab it, but it's too slippery, slick with her saliva. Her body pulses with the pain of my fumbling attempts. I cut a strip from my boardies and use it to grip the tooth, but again it slips off.

I'm getting desperate. I think of my trips to the dentist and it dawns on me they use compressed air to dry people's teeth, so I lean in close and blow into her mouth. There's a ripple of surprise through the audience and I realise it must look like some crazy witch-doctor shit but Eda says nothing so I keep going, taking deep breaths and blowing a jet into her mouth, while trying not to touch her lips with mine.

The gloss disappears from her tooth. I cut another strip from my boardshorts and try again, and this time I get a decent grip. I look up at Eda and Imbi, and with my spare hand I grip the woman's arm tightly, motioning for them to do the same. I see their muscles tense. Then I wiggle and twist the shit out of the tooth.

She bucks and writhes and an inhuman scream rises from deep within her, but I keep going for all I'm worth. I can see her try to clamp her jaw shut against the woman holding it open. She's winning the battle and just in time I jam in the fingers of my other hand to hold it open.

The tooth is moving well now, and I stop wiggling it and take up the knife, trying to ignore the pleading cries of the woman.

"Hold her still," I pointlessly say to my assistants, as I place the tip of the blade on the tooth. I have one hand on the handle, and another as far down the blade as I can get it without obscuring my view.

Keeping the tip on the tooth, I move the blunt edge to the corner of her mouth and bring the blade flat to the neighbouring tooth. Thank fuck it's on the bottom, and not a wisdom tooth, I think. I push a little, and it flexes. She jerks and trembles, and this time I yell at her. She stops. I have to make this quick. I push hard on the tooth with the point of the knife and lever it upwards against its neighbour. I twist the blade to lift it even higher, and I see the tooth rise up out of its socket. More pus spills out and she screams again but I keep going, praying the knife point doesn't slip.

Finally I think I've detached the tooth from whatever's holding it in there, and I put down the knife, reach in again and grab it. I twist it, hard, and pull up and I feel it release and detach itself from the bone and then it's there in my hand and I hold it up to show the crowd, half expecting a cheer.

Eda and Imbi have let the woman go and she springs to her feet, whimpering and spitting blood and pus from her mouth. I mime drinking water to Imbi and point to the woman, and Imbi fetches her a tube and she drinks and spits, drinks and spits, moaning each time the water touches the exposed nerve. I can't think what else to do for her, so instead I turn to Eda and give a thumbs up. He smiles at me.

After the dental work, I breath a little easier, but I know I'm only as good as my last procedure. I feel like one of those crazy fuckers who wear white coats and sneak into hospitals to pretend they're doctors. I know it won't be long until I'm found out, when I fuck something up.

That afternoon I take a walk on the island. Imbi and all of the kids in the village follow me, but no one tries to stop me. My guess is that they don't think I'll leave, because no one has ever left.

I head south and within ten minutes I notice canoes among the trees and then I'm on the beach. It's dazzlingly bright after the jungle and it feels good to stand in the sun. I turn left, east, and walk along the coarse sand, enjoying the feeling of it on my feet, until I reach the rocks and stop. The children clamber around on them, but they're too sharp for me.

It's when I look out to sea and scan the outer reef that I realise where I am. I spot the pass, and on each side the mirror-image surf, spinning across the reef, two muscular arms reaching across the deep water to each other, but never quite meeting. It's three to four feet, and fanned by the sweetest offshore breeze.

I walk back into the jungle and find that there's a well-trodden path through the trees just inland from the rocky point. I follow it for about five hundred metres and sure enough it leads to the beach on the other side of the rocks. There are a couple of outrigger canoes pulled up under the trees.

I walk towards the beach, and through the trees I get a glimpse of waves that would make any surfer weak at the knees. They're mass-produced, perfected and replicated, each a fully-formed masterpiece rising from a turquoise ocean. Feeling the draw of the reef, they stand tall and then fold like closing envelopes, reconstructing themselves into playful, sparkling cylinders which fire down the line. It's the stuff of my dreams. I sit in the sand and simply watch. Imbi sits a few metres away and watches me.

The kids charge into the lagoon for a swim and it's then that I notice the white sword of my surfboard. It's two hundred metres out – halfway to the reef – floating like a leaf on a pond. By some miracle it must have snagged on the coral, stopping the offshore breeze from sending it to oblivion.

There's something about its man-made shape, the familiarity of it, that puts me back into my own domain, bolsters me, gives me the confidence to go after it without asking Imbi for permission.

I wade into the lagoon with the kids, who stop their horsing to watch me go by. When I reach the coral, I swim. It feels good to be in the water, enveloped by its silky warmth, weightless. The scars on my feet cease to hurt, my deprived stomach stops grumbling. I suspect that Imbi might be following me in one of the canoes, but when I flip over and look back towards the beach she's still sitting on the sand, staring after me. I keep going.

When I reach my surfboard, I see that the leggie's still attached, and it's wrapped around a coral head as big as a deer's antler. I unwind it as carefully as I can and see that it's been ground away badly on one side.

I flip the board over and over, and apart from some yellowing in the sun, it looks just fine. It's been lying upside down in the water, so the wax is unmelted, thick and ridged by the wax comb that I used on it little more than a week ago. I remember tossing the comb into the bottom of the boat, and I suddenly get an image of it sloshing around in the seawater and fish blood, occasionally floating out from under a seat and reminding Firoz of the dumb fuck who threw his life away. I wonder what he told Tala when he got back that evening, and what he did with my stuff.

I slide the board under me. I'm going to paddle back into the beach, but a recklessness comes over me and instead I turn and head for the reef. Risk assessment calculations prickle across my forehead as I stroke out through the pass, and every now and again I look back to the beach. Imbi has disappeared, and my heart's in my mouth until I see her again, hauling an outrigger to the water's edge with three of the kids.

This time I head for the right. There's a bit of east in the wind, and a riffle builds across the channel towards the left, but the right is cut glass. Now that I'm closer I see that it doesn't break quite as uniformly as it seemed from the beach. It has imperfections, variety, a slabbing, warping section down the line that holds the promise of a backdoor barrel.

Imbi's halfway out to me by the time I catch my first wave, and I hear the kids squeal in surprise as I get to my feet. It's a beautiful, playful wall and I race along it, a kaleidoscope of colour unfurling beneath my feet. It's so clear that I see a fish darting away as it senses the pull of the wave. In a slower section I whack it a couple of times, and then set up for the backdoor racetrack I know is coming. It doesn't disappoint. The wave gathers itself, heaves upright and a sudden surge of power lifts the back of my board and slingshots me forward. I grip the rail and trail my arm in the face. A gleaming tongue of water rears and throws itself over me as I fizz across the shallowest part of the reef. Even at three foot it's an intimidating section, but I knife through, unscathed, my head buzzing with the sensation.

As I crest out over the back of the wave I look across at Imbi. She's no more than twenty metres away, bobbing in the channel, hanging on to Baka, who's plainly confused at what he's seen.

The other two kids are hyped, bouncing around on their bare arses and shouting. Imbi stares across at me and it's hard to tell what she's thinking, whether she's fascinated or angry that I paddled out here.

I give the kids a wave, turn and head back up the reef. Imbi keeps pace, paddling alongside in the channel. Waves pour through in a seemingly endless set and I'm frothing, paddling hard to get to the take-off spot.

I time my arrival out the back with an absolute gem, and I turn and paddle, my arms burning. It threatens to go without me, but I scramble hard, and manage to lever my board down just enough to catch it. Then I'm away again, searing across the face in a series of high-line speed carves. I send a good chunk of the wave skyward and I hear the kids scream in response. This time I set up even deeper for the barrel and it slabs gratifyingly as I jam my arm harder into the wave. Daylight recedes, and I let go of the wave, bringing all my weight to my front foot, stamping on the gas. I feel the back of the board buck and I fight it, hanging on by my heels. Then, miraculously, the wave seems to rewind, the entrance now coming back to meet me. I explode out of the barrel like a bullet from a gun, a welter of spray bursting out around me.

I surf a dozen more waves before I run out of steam. I'm so tired that I can't climb into the outrigger, and Imbi has to tow me in. The kids stare at me the whole way back to the beach, and I wonder what they're thinking, how they must see me and what they think of what I've just done. I'm suddenly struck by the influence I must be having. I might have dropped in from outer space: I can walk on water – it doesn't get any more mystical than that. It's a powerful realisation that everything I do here will have an effect that might endure for generations. I've planted a seed which will now grow in a way that I have no control over. It won't end well; I'm sure of it, I'm positive. I should be doing everything in my power to leave. But like a hopeless junkie, by the time we reach the shore I've already justified it to myself. I decide to stay for a while, maybe a week, to see how things pan out, maybe to surf the reef a couple more times.

Chapter 15

Eda wakes me up early the next morning. I'm sore with sunburn and trembling with hunger. After my surf yesterday Imbi gave me nothing but raw fish and some chewy, fibrous root which tasted of dirt. It didn't even touch the sides, but when I asked for more she simply stared at me and walked away. I saw the fish the men brought back yesterday afternoon, and there wasn't enough fresh for the village, let alone any left over to dry.

I can tell Eda's worked up about something. He grabs my arm and pulls me out of the hut, and I start to freak that's there some sort of medical emergency I won't know what to do with. The whole village is waiting in the clearing and I desperately look them over to see who's injured.

In the dim light my surfboard stands out like a beacon against the black of their bodies. It's held by one of the men, who must have grabbed it from behind my hut where I stashed it. He holds it away from himself, like it's an evil spirit he's been burdened with, and when I take it from him he visibly relaxes.

Eda says something and points towards the ocean and I know then that he wants to see me walk on water, that Imbi or the kids have told him what they saw.

I mimic eating, but he's having none of it and we set off. I feel weak and nauseous. The entire village follows us through the jungle to the beach, and the men pull the outriggers down the sand to the water. The women and kids stay on the beach.

I get into one of the canoes with Eda and three other men, because I'm not sure I can make the paddle. We're overloaded to fuck, the gunwale only just clearing the water. I have no idea if any of them can swim. The other canoes are the same, laden with men, all keen to see the show.

As we get out into the channel, I'm relieved to see whitewater on the reefs. It's dropped a little from yesterday, but there are still some shapely three-foot runners whizzing their way across the coral. Just as we make it out to the left the sun peeps over the horizon and transforms the swells into lustrous, shimmering strips of gold leaf. It's a mesmerising sight, and I forget my hunger.

Eda orders the canoe too close, and I hurriedly jump off before we get swamped. I pull myself on to my board and paddle, and already I can hear them talking to each other, analysing everything.

I get to the take-off spot and the cool water has revived me a bit. Perfectly formed pieces of ocean are coming at me, and I let the first two go, waiting for something bigger. It's a slightly different wave at this size; gone is the mushing, roll-in take-off, and the wave is more uniform in the speed at which it breaks.

I turn and go on the third wave of the set, and I can hear Eda's shout from the boat as I get to my feet. It's a little beaut of a wave, a perfect quarter-pipe scoop endlessly rising up before me. I go to work on it, hucking reo after reo along the face. I spy the opportunity for a little shack, but it pinches and I get clipped and rolled, right in front of the peanut gallery. When I pop up I look across at them and the expressions on their faces is something I'll remember for the rest of my life. They're freaked.

They're struggling to believe what they've seen. I grin at them and wave, but as I'm paddling back out the feeling comes again to me that I've modified something, that I've changed or damaged these people with a single action. I feel like a character in a time-travel movie, changing something in the past that will forever alter the future.

Eda wants to see more. He yells to me and gesticulates at the waves. I paddle back out and turn for another one, and this time I ease off on the hacks, taking a bit more time to set up the barrel. I'm deep when it starts to throw, and I pump hard and draw up, setting a line high on the face. I'm enveloped in a shimmering golden tunnel, a glossy bobsleigh track. I'm flying through it, my hands carelessly trailing behind my back. It seems to alter, to mould itself around me, to cocoon me. I travel through it for a long time, perhaps six seconds, the spinning disc of its opening like a portal to an otherworldly place. Then it slows, and as I fly out of it I see myself through their eyes; a miracle, like a baby being born.

Before my board even comes off the plane, Eda dives off the canoe and is swimming towards me in a manic doggy-paddle, a mad glint in his eyes. He's not a great swimmer, but he makes it across to the reef and stands up. He yells to me. He wants a go.

I paddle close to him, and he jumps out to me and I help him onto the board. He wobbles, but stays on, and as he thrashes up the reef his legs part and all I can see is his meat and two veg sliding about on the deck of my board as I breaststroke along behind him. He gets knocked off by the whitewater a few times but drags himself back on and keeps going. I shout at him and gesture to come deeper into the channel and paddle around the breaking waves and it takes him a while to understand but eventually he does what I tell him.

It takes him almost ten minutes to get to the top of the point, and I can see that he's getting knackered, but there's no way he's not having a crack. A set goes by and I stop him from paddling into it until he's caught his breath.

The next one that rolls in I push him into. He doesn't stand a chance, and as the board leaves my hand I realise that this might be some sort of humiliation in front of the tribe that he'll blame me for.

I see the yellow soles of his feet disappear as he's sucked over the falls and I wait to see his head bob up in the whitewater, but to my surprise he doesn't appear. I start to wonder if he's gone headfirst into the reef. But then there's a cheer from the canoes and I realise that he's made the drop on his guts and is riding in on the whitewater. All of a sudden he appears, his head rising above the froth, and I can't believe what I'm seeing as he clambers to his feet. The board weaves crazily under him, but he holds on long enough to raise his arms over his head and scream in triumph and the volume doubles from the channel. Then he's down, and when he bobs back up I see he's opened up his arm on the coral but he doesn't even look at it. He's grinning from ear to ear like a grommet after his first ride on a foamy.

I push him into two more before he's had enough, and he gets up both times. The last ride he stays on until the fins hit the coral and he simply steps off onto it. When he comes back to me I flip the board over to examine the fins, and they're a little mashed up but they're fine. I try to explain to him that he shouldn't go on to the reef but I've no idea if he understands or not. He's alive with pleasure, his face like a child's. He hoots as he doggy-paddles back to the canoe, and when I try to get on he pushes me away, pointing to the waves, and I have to ride a dozen more before he's satisfied enough to allow me back on board.

All the way back to shore Eda never stops talking. His men are also in a state of high animation, chattering away to each other. They're talking about my board and running their hands over it, inspecting the fins, tugging on the leggie. They look at me differently – I've gained the chief's favour. But the bloke I rugby-tackled, who Eda slammed in the throat, sits up in the bow and doesn't say a word. He stares at me with a cold hatred that makes my hair stand on end.

Near the shore, one of the men cries out and leaps off the boat into the shallows. When he pops up he's holding a huge hawksbill turtle by its shell, its flippers windmilling ridiculously in the air. It's so big he's barely able to hang onto it, and two other men jump in to help. They drag the creature up on to the beach and drive their knives in under its shell and it goes limp immediately.

Eda gives an order and the men butcher it then and there. The whole village gathers around to watch, and there's a ripple of excited conversation when they see the eggs pulled from its body and piled into the upturned shell.

One of the women says something to the children and they fan out across the beach, on the hunt for something. It's not long until one of them returns with a shell as big as his hand. It's given to one of the men, who fills it with turtle blood and hands it to Eda. There's a reverent silence while he speaks, and then he raises the shell to his lips and drinks it.

The shell is passed forward and refilled, and the man who was staring at me in the boat is just about to drink from it when Eda takes it from him and hands it to me. I look at the guy, and I can see he's furious, but he doesn't protest.

Eda's blood-stained smile is giving me the shits, but there's no way I'm going to refuse him. I'm also so hungry I'd eat anything. I put it to my lips, and I can smell the richness, the salty potency. It's thick, almost slimy, and I swallow it the way I'd swallow an oyster. Eda nods at me, and then orders the rest of the village to drink. There's a shell-full of blood for everyone, before any of the eggs or flesh are touched. Then it's a free-for-all. I join in, ignoring my revulsion. The eggs pop and run, the flesh is chewy and tough. There's blood running down my chin, splattered on my chest. The food revives me, fills my belly. There's still not enough of it, but I instantly feel better.

Afterwards Eda and the men go off fishing so I spend the rest of the day with the women. Imbi digs for roots and tubers, and I watch her, trying to figure out how she knows where to dig.

She uses a digging adze, with a branch for a handle, and a chunk of steel for the blade. Whenever I can, I steal some of whatever Imbi's dug up and gnaw on it.

The women often sing together, and to my ears it's a tuneless drone, rising and falling without any kind of melody. But it's an exotic soundtrack to the day. The children follow us about, gallivanting in the jungle, climbing trees and vines. They snack on red ants, falling on a nest like hyenas taking to a carcass. It's impossible to know which children belong to which woman – they seem not to discriminate when they want something. When they get tired, they simply find a log to lie on and fall asleep like leopards in a tree.

I've figured out the word for name – 'lem' – and I say it to her all day, asking the words for anything I see. She must think I'm stupid; I ask the names of the same things over and over before they stick. But gradually I get a small vocabulary of the essentials going.

The mozzies are ripping into me and Imbi sends a girl back to the village for a shell full of the yellow repellant. We move on through the jungle and I see Imbi bending over branches and folding leaves into roots on the ground and when the girl comes back I realise Imbi was leaving a trail for her to follow. I cover my chest and arms and legs, and Imbi rubs it over my back. Immediately I'm left alone. Later Imbi points to a pale plant in the jungle, then touches my back to let me know it's the one she makes the repellant from. She hacks off the leaves and ties them in a bundle, telling me the name which I'm doubtful I'll ever be able to pronounce.

We roam far and wide across the island. The jungle doesn't let up, and compared to the women I'm like a bull in a China shop. I crash and trip and stumble my way through it and it's stifling hot and I'm getting more and more pissed off. But then I hear the kids squealing up ahead and we come out of the trees to the edge of a watering hole in the middle of the jungle. I can't believe my eyes. It's crystal clear, and the kids are running along the bank and leaping into its shallow end. At the other it's so deep that I can't see the bottom, just a blue-green portal into the abyss.

The women drop everything on the side of the pool and plunge in with the children, who are squealing and hooting. I just stand and stare. It's a scene of such joyous abandon that I find myself smiling like a fool.

The trees all around grow out over the pool, and I scramble up the trunk of one whose branches hang over the deep end. The kids go quiet as I get higher, sensing a trick. I give them a bit of a show, bombing off it to make the biggest splash I can. Underwater, it's a tonic, cool and silky, and I stay there for a bit, feeling the cold seep into my body, letting it do its work on my jungle-frazzled mind.

When I pop up, the kids are already out of the water and running around the bank to the base of the tree I climbed. They zip up the trunk and gather on the branch I leapt from like pigeons on a power line. They're chattering and poking each other and laughing and I can see the fear on some of their faces as they contemplate the dark depths below me.

An older boy is the first to go, and it's only when he pops up and then immediately goes back under again that I realise he can't swim and I'm the lifeguard. I grab him and shunt him across the pool until he can touch the ground. Then the next kid jumps, and I've got to race to get him.

There are some older kids who can doggy-paddle their way to safety, but the rest of them I have to rescue. A couple of times two jump in at once and it's a job to pull them both out. I tell them one at a time, and the women call out to them and there's only a little more order to the chaos.

One by one, the kids drop out of the game and sit on the bank to rest. Now there's only some of the older boys left and they can take care of themselves, and I'm just about to make for the side when Imbi appears on the branch. She shuffles along it until she's right above me. I swim away to give her space, but she gestures and calls me back and I realise that she can't swim and wants me to help. So I wait, treading water, while she plucks up the courage.

She doesn't make a sound as she drops into the water, but she comes up spluttering and when I swim to her she clings like a limpet and tries to climb me like a tree. I'm laughing as she pushes me under. I grovel my way across the pool until my toes touch the bottom.

Now I'm aware of her small breasts in my face, her nipples brushing my cheek. I have one hand on her waist and another on her arse as I carry her up the rock to the shallows. She's still clinging to me tightly and her breath comes quickly with the exhilaration of her jump, but when she realises we've reached safety she slides down my body and I know she can feel me, and she looks down. I'm mortified, and I turn away quickly and splash back into the deeper part of the pool, and Imbi climbs out. I see her say something to the other women, and they cackle like Coolangatta housewives and I know she's told them.

When I get my shit together I make my way back to the shallows and lie on my back on the smooth rock, enjoying the sensation of actually getting a chill. Baka, Imbi's boy, wades back in and splashes me and then jumps up on to my chest. Since he saw me surfing he's taken to following me around like he's my shadow. He never stops talking, keeping up a full commentary for me even though he knows I can't understand him. He's a determined little fucker. He screams at Imbi when he doesn't get his way. He's hardy and tough. I saw him kick a rock at a full sprint and just get up and keep going, limping as he ran.

In the late afternoon Imbi shows me how to crush the leaves of the plant we collected, grinding them into a paste with a stone on a scalloped rock. We then squeeze out the oil, dripping it carefully into the mouth of spiral shells, which she stoppers with the remaining fibre. She hands all the shells to me and I line them up carefully against the wall in the hut.

When the men return from fishing and hunting I'm on edge when I see Imbi go up to Eda. I'm shitting myself she's going to tell him about me in the swimming hole. But either she doesn't tell him or he's not worried about it because he smiles at me from across the clearing.

Chapter 16

It's the next morning that I decide that I'm going to ditch my boardies. They're ripped and filthy, and I reckon that when I do leave, I'm going to need them. Plus, without any undies they're chafing like fuck in very unwelcome places. I bundle them up and jam them under a rafter in the hut and rub the repellant carefully over my groin and arse.

I'm expecting a bit of a stir when I walk into the clearing, but it's fair to say that what I get exceeds my expectations. I'm inspected and discussed in great detail by every member of the village, and it's so intrusive I'm close to curling up in the foetal position. They show no embarrassment as they gather around me; men, women and children. Eda is still sleeping, but someone wakes him up to see what the fuss is about. There are long conversations held, and when one of the women reaches out to touch it I draw the line and bugger off into the jungle for a bit of peace.

I hear the roar of the ocean long before I reach the beach, and when I emerge from the trees the air is charged with the salt tang of sea spray. It's overcast, the sky studded with bruise-coloured clouds.

Out on the reef, colossal waves lurch and grind and topple like roadtrains overturning on a slate-grey highway. They're at least fifteen feet, and seem to break in slow motion, a fresh south-easterly onshore pushing over their tops and triggering seething avalanches of whitewater down their laddered faces.

I see immediately that the reef has reached its limits; the waves sense some submarine feature out in the channel, and the resultant bombora mushes across the deep water until it meets the oncoming wave. The waves themselves have lost the reef, breaking too far off the coral to hold their shape.

I sit on the sand watching for a while, awed by the power of the ocean. And then, like any surfer, I start to analyse it, figuring out the swell direction and wind, and my eyes are drawn to the west.

I've stashed my board in the trees, and I grab it and start to walk. It's hard going on the beach; the rocks are murder on my feet, but I discover that the inland track I found in the jungle back from the point continues right around the island. It's smooth and well-trodden, and it's always only a short trot back out to the beach.

As I make my way around the coast I see two small reef passes, both of which look promising, but are overwhelmed today by the slabs of water heaving themselves into them. It's smaller here, but still a good eight to ten feet.

Each time I peep out of the jungle, the waves are smoothed more and more by the wind; cross-shore, cross-off, and then finally offshore as I reach the western-most point of the island. There's another pass, bigger than the last two, and I walk more quickly, and then start to jog as I see a wave bend into it and a plume of spray rise up from its breaking crest. I keep my eyes on it as I stumble along the beach and the plume travels for a long time, finally dying away deep in the pass. Another wave follows, then another.

I have to cut back inland as there's hardly any beach left, and I all but sprint the last bit of the track. When I come back out of the jungle I'm floored by the sight of it: it's a freight train. A four-hundred-metre race track. It's hard to tell just how big it is from this distance, but I guess at about six to eight foot as I wade out into the lagoon. The coral and sand alternate the whole way out, and I shunt my way over to save my arms. But as I get closer, I can't contain myself and I jump on and start to paddle like I'm in a priority battle with Gabriel Medina. I'm hyperventilating as I paddle up the point, gasping with disbelief at the waves pouring along the reef towards me. I have to stop myself from turning and catching the end of them; they're siren-like, sinuous and tempting.

The wave's a barrel from beginning to end, rearing and hauling itself up and over the shallowest reef I've ever seen. It's like Kandui's, but twice the length. There'll be no re-entries, no cutbacks.

Out the back I get a measure of the size. There are some solid sets. Great silver walls turn into the pass like gates swinging on a fencepost. Some of the bigger ones start to cream up the point and rumble down, but there's a clear-cut delineation when they hit the reef. They turn themselves inside out. The crack as the lip strikes the flats turns my insides to liquid. Compressed air forces itself through the back of the wave in jets and spurts, the vaporised sea water speeding away on the wind.

I consider trying to catch the mush further up, but there's a risk of being too deep when the thing jacks, so I watch for a while to get the best take-off point nailed.

I choose my spot and paddle in. I turn and paddle for the first two waves of the next set that arrives, but pull back both times, the image of the blue-green reef rising up to meet me still dancing in front of my eyes. It's insanely shallow. The fact that I'm butt-naked only makes it worse.

I sit, fidgeting, cursing myself, and in the lull it doesn't seem so critical, but when the next one rears it's an eight-foot bomb and I realise that it gets thicker as it gets bigger. It sucks so hard off the reef that it lowers the sea level, a warping trench through which I can only travel in my imagination. The rest of the set is the same, and I scratch over them all, each time making the mistake of looking down into the abyss. I swear it's getting bigger.

I'm breathing hard after that, trying to rid myself of the adrenaline that's spurting through me. I feel stiff and my jaw seems locked in place. I'm transfixed by the wave's power, and haunted by the awful thought that I know it's rideable, but perhaps not by me. I know that these could be the best waves I've ever seen, but I'm terrified by the idea that I might not catch one.

I'm under-gunned, that's for sure. I wait for a more manageable set, and when I see it coming I smack my fist into my chest and yell at it, psyching myself up. It works. It heaves and warps beneath me and I can feel its power coming from somewhere far back in its bulk. I stroke early and hard, and I don't even look down until I'm on my feet, and then all my bravado evaporates as the bottom drops out of the wave. It's wildly fast. The wall seems to go from the horizontal to the vertical with the most perfunctory of connecting ramps.

Somehow I make the drop and turn ahead of the thundering curtain. My feet aren't in the right place, and I skitter madly along the face, deprived of any control by the sheer brutality of the wave. I scramble to set my feet and get it together just in time to sneak under the lip, which is leaving without me. I'm racing, flat to the boards, all my weight to the front, and in the second it takes for my board to respond I drift back into the tunnel and brace for the violent flick I know is coming. But, somehow, the moment elongates, then elongates again, and suddenly I'm at warp speed, screaming through the spiralling mess, half-blinded by spray. The wave throws in sections, great glass slabs sliding overhead, always distressingly far ahead. But the speed I'm travelling at is new to me, and it renders the impossible possible. A lion is snapping at my heels, but it can't quite catch me.

I can scarcely believe it when I emerge out on to the face, my board thrumming under me. For a moment I relax, but again I see the wave rear – appallingly far down the line – and the water thins beneath my feet, throwing the flying carpet of coral beneath into stark relief. My heart leaps back into my mouth as again I hurtle headlong into the tunnel. Everything moves so fast that I can only react instinctively. I battle the wave, fighting against it, but my adjustments are too clumsy and fractions too slow. Like a teenage driver oversteering on a gravel road, my mistakes compound, and I don't make the barrel. I'm collected by the wall and sent into space with breathtaking speed. Up and over I go, and there's no question of curling into a ball for the inevitable impact on the reef. I'm helpless, stretched on the rack of the lip, and it's with a kind of hypnotic fascination that I go over the falls. The danger is awful, but there's a certain resignation to not being able to do anything about it.

I have a miracle wipeout, the kind you'd breathlessly tell your mates about afterwards. I must have met the water rebounding back up off the reef because my plummet is slowed, stopped, reversed. I don't even touch the coral. Somehow I slip between the spinning vortexes and the violent turbulence and I'm deposited in the spritzing foam out the back of the wave as gently as a parent lays a child in its cot. In a panic I search for my board, believing that there must have been some price to pay, but there it is, floating beside me, in one piece. I can't believe it, and I start to laugh as I paddle back out for another.

I rode five waves that day, each bigger than the last, before my leggie snapped. Number four I'll remember forever; a gaping, galloping, stretching mineshaft that I thought would never end, but seemed to go by in an instant. It splintered the light, warped time. When I was blown out into the channel, I skimmed fifteen metres out on the flats before I finally came off the plane, grinning like a lunatic.

Chapter 17

There are nine waves on the island.

There's the two out from the beach on either side of the pass, which I call 'Mine' and 'Yours', their names alternating depending on which one of them I decide to surf that day. 'Freights' is the name I've given to the big racetrack barrel, and I discover that there's another one even further north, a long, wrapping lefthander that, too, goes like the clappers, which is why I called it that.

The two little reef passes I spotted on my walk to Freights are almost identical; playful, short lefts I've christened 'Thing One' and 'Thing Two'.

There's a bizarre novelty wave close to Thing One that I missed on the day I first surfed Freights. It begins before it begins, when a refracting wave rebounds sideways off the reef and meets the next one in the set, throwing up a teepee which launches itself skyward. Waist-high waves momentarily turn into well overhead, critical take-offs, and it's anyone's guess what's going to happen next. It warps and lurches, barrels and goes fat. I've called it 'The Freakshow', and it's low-risk and pure fun.

East of Mine is another decent pass where the men often leave from to go fishing. There's a left and a right. They're the last two waves that I discover and I can't believe it took me more than two weeks to find them. The pass faces slightly more east, so picks up less swell than Mine. Both are quality waves. The right is a fifty-metre nugget that hauls itself up out of the ocean like a sea lion onto a rock, slabbing as wide as it is tall. Blowing the take-off is an awful, frightening experience, but making the barrel is like being ejected from a cannon. I've called it 'Heartstopper'.

On the other side of the pass, the left is a different beast altogether, a sidewinding, sinuous beauty breaking well down into the bay. It's the most user-friendly wave on the island, all long, whispering walls and almond-shaped barrels. I've called it 'Mum's'.

I've never had the honour of naming a wave in my life before, but now I'm even naming sections. There's 'The Rifle', 'The Cheesegrater', 'The Closer', 'Skingraft Alley', 'Fishfood Reef'. The names come to me in the ceaseless babble I keep up whenever I'm not with Imbi or the kids aren't around. I seem to have a compelling urge to fill the silence with something, and I talk incessantly as I wander along the beach or the inland tracks, my board tucked under my arm. I ask questions out loud and then answer them with the gravity of a high court judge. Occasionally I get a glimpse of myself as a visitor might; a naked castaway losing his mind. I've woven a sunhat the size of an umbrella which only adds to the crazy. But the periods between those moments of self-realisation lengthen; most of the time I'm barely aware of how strangely I'm behaving. It's when I return to the village, or when I see Imbi or Eda, or any of the people, that I check myself, like a drunk trying to act like he's sober.

I repair my leggie with the fine strands of dried flax that they make rope with, and it's a decent, strong repair, but the urethane cord's about to go in two other places and it won't be long until it's useless. I try not to think of it, but every time I feel a tug at my ankle I come up expecting to see it broken.

My board is in bad shape. There are pressure dings all over it, and a violent encounter with The Closer removed six inches of nose; the brown stain of the water travelling down into the foam is like an hourglass counting down the seconds of surfing that remain to me. The wax left on the board is paper-thin, and I spend a long time between surfs redistributing it to where it's most needed.

My feet get tougher every day. I can walk over the coral now. My arse goes pink and peels, then goes as brown as the rest of me. I still get sunburnt, though, and unless there's cloud cover I surf only in the mornings and evenings. The middle of the day I spend with the women and kids. I get Imbi to name everything, sticking close by her, and help her to dig out tubers and collect jungle fruit. I haven't marked the time, but I suspect a month has gone by. The pact that I made with myself to stay a week seems like it was made by another person entirely. When he pipes up from time to time, I simply ignore him.

One day I see Imbi cure a kid's hiccups the same way I did, and she does it so expertly that I realise she knew the trick before I ever came along. I ask her, but she either doesn't understand me or pretends not to.

Eda doesn't seem to mind what I do; Imbi must have told him she's teaching me their language and he's obviously cool with it. There's a hierarchy among the men, and I think he's keeping me from it. They fight each other regularly, without weapons, savage brawls in the dirt. They deliver rapid-fire punches at each other with no thought of parrying the blows, and think nothing of delivering a brutal kick. I'm tested one day with a dislocated shoulder when a man named Eto, who's as skinny as a vine, loses a fight to the guy I tackled when I got to the village. His name's Joro, and as I suspected, he's a fuckwit. There's a dark malevolence about him, which often manifests as a cuff across the face of his missus or their daughter, who's about eight. He's one of the bigger men in the village, and he's feared; he's brawny and handy in a fight. I realise that I got lucky that Eda stepped in when he did. Joro isn't much liked by Eda, but he has allies among the younger men. They often sit in a group, talking quietly and glancing up occasionally to locate the subject of their discussion, which is usually me.

Joro's fight with Eto seems to happen without provocation. Joro simply kicks out at him as he walks past. I've got to know Eto a little bit; he's thoughtful and quiet, and in the evenings he often sits beside me and listens patiently as I try out new words on him. He's a plucky scrapper, and doesn't hesitate when Joro kicks him, but the bigger man quickly gets the better of him, grinding his face into the dirt to humiliate him. Joro then grabs Eto's arm and wrenches it up behind his back until there's an audible pop and a scream of pain from Eto, and he struggles to get to his feet. Joro then walks to the other side of the clearing and sits, staring not at Eto, but at me. The village looks on without a word.

Eto comes over to me, leaning forward, his arm dangling useless, his face distorted. I look him in the eyes, and he smiles back at me through his pain. Then I look across at Joro and grin at him because I know I've got this one. Willo dislocated his shoulder at Snapper one day, and a doctor saw him walking up the beach holding it awkwardly and stopped him and put it back in, right there and then. I saw how he did it.

Eto's holding his arm across his stomach and I take it and by pressing down gently on his shoulder and breathing deeply I make him understand that he has to relax. Eda's come out of his hut to watch. I then swing Eto's forearm out like a gate and he winces but he doesn't try to fight it. I hold my breath as I grip his upper arm and pull it forward. Then I bring his forearm back across his body and I feel it click as it drops back into the socket and Eto lets out a sigh. I lie him on his back with his arm across his chest and he's comfortable and quiet.

Joro's still staring at me from across the clearing, so I give him a wink and tell him to get fucked.

Chapter 18

There are more things I do that change this island, these people, each a diversion to their way of life. Some of them are little things, unconsciously done; no one ever thought to bomb off the log before, but now that's all the kids – and Imbi – want to do. It requires me to make a conscious change, a big change; to teach them all to swim, so that no kid ends up drowning in the hole after I'm gone. They're astonished when I swim freestyle. I do laps of the watering hole and they line the banks and cheer me on. So, I show them how, and they practice like crazy. I see them teaching each other, and I realise they'll continue to teach each other forever, long after I'm gone. How the Sentinelese learned to swim freestyle.

Then, one surfless day I decide to see if I can make a fire. I try all morning, rubbing various types of timber together. It's a dismal failure but I see that one type of hardwood generates more heat and I experiment, digging a groove in one piece and then carefully splitting it to allow in some air. I sharpen the end of another piece and rub like crazy and after a while a tiny spire of smoke snakes into the air but it's impossible to keep up the pace and get tinder in place at the same time.

I'm just about to give up when Imbi gives me some dried fish and I'm so sick of the taste of it that it motivates me to keep going. In the evening when the men return I get Eto to help me. By this stage I've remembered a doco I saw where they made fire with an instrument like a violin bow. I've made one from some wood and thin flax rope, and the bowstring runs once around a short piece of the hardwood which I've sharpened to a point at one end. It fits in a groove I've dug out from a softer piece on the ground.

I get Eto to hold the stick at the top while I pull the bow back and forth. Eto can't hold it, but he's figured out what I want. He gets another piece and digs a hole in it for the top of the stick to go into, and it looks like it's going to work. I get going on the bow again and it spins like a champ. In just a few seconds smoke starts to curl up into Eto's face. He freaks and yells to the rest of the village and from then on it's a full-scale show.

The tinder gathered around the base of the stick won't light, but when I pull it away there's a decent ember glowing in the piece on the ground, so I dig it out with a knife and place it into the bundle of tinder and blow. The Sentinelese are spellbound, and there's complete silence until it catches and then they lose the plot, jumping and dancing around the clearing. Eda thumps me repeatedly on the chest, his eyes shining with joy in the flaring flames.

Immediately I see that they know what to do with fire, how to handle it, and soon there's a decent bonfire in the clearing. Eto sits beside me, points at the fire and makes the sound of lightning and thunder and it's then I realise that their only source of fire is naturally occurring, when lightning strikes. Then he says the word for rain, which I know, and sprinkles dirt on a glowing ember at the edge of the fire until it dulls. I understand. It arrives with one storm, and the next takes it away.

How the Sentinelese learned to make fire.

The cuisine improves after that. I cook my raw fish on a stick over the fire, and pretty soon the kids try it, and then the adults. The smoky lumps of firm white flesh are greasy and rich, and the taste brings me back to the Rainbow Bay Surf Club, and I'd do anything for a cold beer to wash it down.

I make the mistake of trapping and killing a bird to eat; my yearning for meat is powerful now I have the means to cook it. But Imbi discovers me plucking out its feathers and cuffs my head, delivering a rapid-fire remonstration. She takes the bird and buries it quickly, continually glancing back towards the village as she does it, checking to see if anyone's coming. When she's finished she stands up and goes at me again, and I don't understand any of the words but the meaning is crystal clear.

I tell myself that the changes I make are improvements, that life for the Sentinelese is better than before I arrived, but the voice of Jess comes to me, telling me like she always does that I'm an expert in self-justification.

And yet, I try to hold the world at bay for them – or for me, I'm not sure which. I pick up the plastic rubbish I find on the beaches; chip packets and nylon fishing ropes and fucking plastic straws. I scratch out a hole with a stick and bury it as deep as I can. I'm infuriated by it, sickened. I've seen the Sentinelese walk right past the rubbish; they won't touch it. Sometimes, before I fall asleep, I think of it in its island grave, and even the idea of it tainting the earth gives me the shits. The irony is of course that I'm the biggest pollutant of all.

One day Imbi sends Baka back to the village with the other women and children and leads me through the jungle to the far north of the island. I don't know where we're going and can't figure out what she's telling me so I just trot along behind her. The silent woman I knew is now long gone; she chatters away to me as we go, and I pick up words here and there, but she doesn't seem to need to impress on me the meaning of what she's saying, and the sound of her voice is soothing. But when Imbi talks about food, she gets more animated. She says the word for fish, and then suddenly she stops and tries to explain something. She mimics a fish with her arm, and then flings it away out to sea. She says the word for none, for nothing, and the word for food again, and points back towards the village. I finally twig that she's telling me the fishing is bad, that they can't catch enough for the people to eat. She's upset. She looks at me for a while and I stare back at her. Thoughts cross her face like clouds scudding across the sun. Then she turns and keeps walking.

I think about what she says as I go. The men catch their fish with bows and arrows, two-metre-long shafts that they fire from their canoes. The first time I saw it I couldn't believe it. They lash mats of branches together and tie them in place around the reef as fish-aggregating devices, then surround them in their canoes and wait for the fish to swim out into the open. They're unbelievably accurate, able to skewer them a metre underwater, but it still doesn't make for a bountiful catch.

As we get further north, the jungle gives way to sparse vegetation. It's strange to be able to move through it easily. We make our way onto the hook of a peninsula, following a well-worn track.

Imbi stops and points. I look up, and I'm floored. My body actually jolts with shock. I can't believe what I'm seeing. The wreck of a hulking freighter ship juts out of the water, stranded on the reef just inside the pass, and it's a weird rush that pulses through me at the sight of it. I'm suddenly afraid, and involuntarily, stupidly, I look around me, scanning for the ship's crew, emerging from the scrub, guns raised.

Imbi trots towards it without fear. We get closer and I see that its hull is well rusted, that it's been here for years, decades maybe. I try to ask Imbi how long, but she doesn't understand my question.

We skirt along the side of the ship and I can still see the name of it on the bow – The Primrose. We wade through the water, working our way towards the lowest part of the gunwale. The ship is listed well over on to its side here, and I help Imbi up and then climb up over the gunwale myself.

It's an eerie place. A steel mausoleum. There's a weight to it, a palpable maleficence. I wonder did the Sentinelese slaughter the survivors?

I say the word for men to Imbi, and she looks at me strangely and says something I don't understand. She uses a word I've heard all the villagers use a lot – 'biyase' – but I haven't been able to figure out what it means.

Imbi makes her way along the deck towards the bow. The stern and the bow of the ship are well clear of the sea, but the centre sags enough to lie beneath the water, like the hull has broken in half. I can see the bridge at the stern, and wonder if there are the bones of men in there, an islander's arrow lying among them.

Imbi seems to know where she's going. We reach the bow and she goes to the shredded mess of steel plating where the ship must have struck the reef. It has rusted through in places, leaving evil blades of ochre-hued steel poking out in all directions. Imbi grips one and starts working it back and forth. It's so rusted along its length that it bends easily, and she soon has it snapped off. She lays it on the deck and starts on another one.

I realise suddenly that this is where the steel for the Sentinelese tools comes from – their knives and adzes and digging tools. I tap Imbi on the shoulder and point at the digging tool in her waistband and then back at the steel and she nods, smiling at me. She says the word 'biyase' again, and I twig what it means – their god. The steel is a gift from god.

We work away at the steel until there's a pile on the deck, and then I try to convince Imbi to swim out to the stern of the ship for a look inside the bridge. But she's reluctant, so I go alone. It's a job getting up to it, and rust patches threaten to collapse under me.

I go into the bridge with my heart in my mouth but there are no bones on the floor, just rocks. It makes me smile because the glass has been smashed out from the windows and I think that kids are the same wherever you go. The weather and salt have wreaked havoc inside. There's nothing obvious to be salvaged, but Imbi's fossicking has given me an idea. I'm in need of some tools for my medical practice. I tried to help Eto with an ingrown toenail a few days before but the knife was too clumsy and I worried I'd slice open his foot so we gave up and I hoped for the best. I need something more delicate.

I take up the biggest rock from the floor of the bridge and bash at a casing from the instrument panel until it comes away. I get a fright when a rusty old fork clatters to the floor; it must have been sitting in the groove above the casing. I stare at it for a moment and it gives me an idea and so I pick it up.

Removing the casing reveals a circuit board underneath. I eye the two brackets holding it, thinking that I can sharpen them to make small blades, and I break away the circuit board and bend the brackets back and forth until they come away. I also pull out the wires underneath. The ends have corroded away but I figure that the copper inside the plastic casing might be intact and could be useful.

When I get back to Imbi she's sitting on a rock, waiting for me. I sit down beside her and she looks at my haul with interest, examining each item carefully. She's intrigued by the colourful wire, it's pliability and strength. She murmurs away quietly to herself and I watch the thoughts travel across her expressive face. Then she binds everything up with flax and we set off.

Imbi and I stop at the watering hole on the way back and she wants to jump in the deep end so makes me go in first to rescue her. When she surfaces she grabs for me and I laugh as she climbs up me again, pulling me under. I can't seem to make her understand that she needs to keep only her head out of the water and I try to pull her down but she's having none of it so I doggy-paddle across the pool swallowing water until I can touch the rock. Still she clings to me and she's smooth and curvy and again there's nothing I can do to hide the effect it's having on me.

Imbi stands back and studies me with a smile on her face and I stand there mortified until she steps back to me and takes my cock in her hand and I can't help but let out a groan. She talks to me softly as she walks out of the water and up the bank.

I try to kiss her, but she doesn't understand what I'm doing. Instead I kiss her neck, her chest, her breasts. She gives out little sighs of pleasure and we lie down on the moss, and she guides me inside her and I'm like an escaped convict I want her so badly. We fuck with a frantic urgency.

When Imbi and I get back to the village I busy myself sharpening the brackets so that I can operate on Eto's toe when he gets back from fishing but also to take my mind off what's just happened. I shit myself whenever I see Imbi talking to the other women, sure that she's telling them what we did. I don't know what I've done, what protocols I've breached.

When Eda comes back to the village, he goes to his hut and I see Imbi standing at his door talking to him and I wait for him to come out, enraged, his stone club gripped in his hand. But I see Imbi walk away and I can see Eda's feet through the doorway. He's resting. I don't know what to think, so to take my mind off it I call Eto over and have a go at his toe. It's a job cutting his toenail, but with one bracket I lift it and with the other I shave away at the edge until it's well free of the skin. He grimaces through it but doesn't move a muscle. It's infected, so I pack some of Imbi's green paste into it. He's delighted, and stands in front of me silently, his hands on my shoulders, to say thanks.

Eda emerges for his dinner and he simply looks at me and smiles and there's no sign that he knows or cares.

I figure that Imbi has decided to keep it a secret so when she comes into my hut at first light the next morning I get a shock. I point outside, my eyes wide, but she's unfazed.

Imbi has obviously been thinking about how I kissed her, because she puts her lips to mine and it takes a little while but she gets the hang of it. She explores with her mouth, sucking gently on my lips. She tastes of earth and of salt. Then she sits astride me and puts her breasts to my mouth and I'm inside her and I'm trying to stay quiet but she's moaning and moving faster and the hut is creaking beneath us until she collapses on top of me. We lie like that silently for a while, her dozing, me listening for activity outside, and then Imbi leaves, stealing away quietly into the morning.

PART THREE

Chapter 19

When Joro sends his huge fishing arrow towards the first Brazo he screams but then it strikes him in the heart and he's instantly silenced. The shaft sticks out grotesquely from his chest, quivering. For a moment the Brazo stares at it, as if confused at how it got there, and then his face contorts and he wheezes and topples slowly off his board.

I paddle as fast as I can after the canoe. I paddle past the dying man, his eyes rolling back, his blood staining the water, and my throat thickens and I hyperventilate, struggling to breathe. I try calling out to Joro, but he already has another arrow notched and he's ordering the canoe up behind the second Brazo. The man's crying and pleading, still paddling hard for their boat.

Joro's drawing out the moment, enjoying the Brazo's fear, and my impotence. It's a strange and awful procession we make. The chased and the chaser, both whimpering and crying out for mercy, while the three men in the canoe are completely silent. The two paddlers keep pace, and Joro now sits astride the bow, his arrow trained on the middle of the Brazo's back.

Joro allows the man to paddle all the way to his boat, which takes more than a minute. He then calmly shoots him just as he tries to haul himself aboard. The Brazo clings onto the gunwale, his chest heaving, but he doesn't cry out. Joro then urges the canoe forward and finishes him with his knife, leaning out of the dugout to stab him in the side of his neck, and the Brazo slides back into the water without a sound, the blood causing a slick across the surface.

It takes me all morning to bury them. The Sentinelese simply left them floating in the pass, their boards floating beside them. They didn't even take their boat. They simply paddled back to shore and hauled their canoes back into the jungle. Joro stared at me as they passed by, but I looked away.

The one by the boat, I had to remove his leggie, wrap it once around the anchor rope and reattach it to his wrist so he didn't float away. Then I went over to the second lad, and I paddled him back to the boat. I tried but I couldn't pull them in, so I just chucked their boards in, then tied them both to the back and towed them in. It was when I was motoring back to shore, staring at their boards and their bags, no longer engaged in the struggle of heaving about their bodies, that it fully hit me and I was a sobbing, snotty mess by the time I reached the beach.

I dragged them up into the trees and I had to rest for a while to sort myself out. I couldn't stop hyperventilating and my heart felt like it was going to leap out of my chest.

I didn't want to pull out the arrows, so I broke them off and threw them away into the jungle. Then I started to dig. I used a stick and scratched away at the ground but there were roots everywhere so I had to go a bit closer to the beach and start again. For hours I scrabbled away at the sand, trying not to look at the two boys lying there in the jungle. Whenever I turned my back it felt like they were watching me.

I got the holes to about a metre down and dragged the boys into them. I was thinking to say a few words but I couldn't stand looking at them there, curled up in their holes, the sand and dirt and grass matting with the congealed blood from their wounds. I pushed the earth over them as quickly as I could and then I sat in the sand and cried.

Sitting here now beside the graves I have an almost uncontrollable urge to dig them up again; that they might still be alive, and I have to stop myself from clawing at the earth with my fingers. Then I'm away, sprinting down the beach and into the water. I lie in it for a long time, and it helps. I take deep breaths and turn face down and listen to the little crackles and pops of the reef and it calms me and I hold my breath for so long that I see stars when I come up.

When I come out of the sea I go over to their boat and stare at it for ages. Their T-shirts are carelessly thrown over the seats where they left them. A phone is tucked inside a baseball cap. Two empty cans of Coke lie in the bottom, floating in a rainbow-hued puddle of seawater and gasoline.

There are two spare petrol tanks, easily enough to get back to Port Blair. I look around and there's still no one on the beach.

Then I spot, tucked under the seat, a first-aid kid. I pull it out and open it. It's well-stocked; bandages, dressings, saline, Steri Strips, even scalpel blades, anaesthetic and sutures. There's a shitload of painkillers and antibiotics and malaria pills.

I pull their boat up the beach as far as I can and throw the anchor up high on the sand. I go through their stuff and they don't have much, and I can't find their passports so I figure that they've got the rest of it at a hotel in Port Blair. I pull on one of the T-shirts and stuff the other into a bag with their boardies and a pair of trainers. There's sunscreen, wax, and a wax comb, and I shove them in the bag. There's a surf hat which I jam on my head. I drink a bottle of water they had stashed up front, and there I find nuts and mangos and I eat them all, pushing the luscious fruit into my mouth until the juice runs down my chin.

I take the outboard motor off the transom and drag it into the jungle, propping it up against a tree. I put the petrol tanks beside it and cover it all with palms.

Then, I take one of the surfboards and stash it in the jungle.

I pick up the other one. It's snow-white, brand new, and it feels good tucked under my arm. Like a programmed robot I check the surf at Mine. It's still absolutely firing. I strap on the leggie. It's new, too, and should last for months if I mind it.

Chapter 20

For weeks after the Brazilians I search the horizon, and occasionally I see the dark dots of ships passing; fishing boats and freighters, but then one morning I spot what looks to be a coastguard type of boat. It's only a couple of kilometres out. That afternoon I'm waxing my new board in the trees and a plane passes overhead. It's only a few hundred metres up and it zips over the beach and then turns and comes back and circles the beach a few times. The Brazos' boat is still there, fully exposed; the Sentinelese won't touch it, not even to destroy it.

I stay back in the trees, watching the plane, telling myself that I'm the reason it's here.

For days after that I expect an armed party to arrive on the island, come to rescue the Brazos, and I've resigned myself that that will be the end of it, that I'll return home with them, tell them the truth about what happened. I prepare myself, rehearsing my story in my head, but nothing happens, no one comes.

A week later, Joro takes his knife and slices open Eto's hand in another unprovoked attack. Joro's naked hostility towards me is expanding outwards, to anyone who's fond of me or spends time with me.

Eto comes running into the village with the fleshy bulb of his palm gaping open, yelling for me. As soon as I see it, I know immediately that the wound is far beyond the connective abilities of a Steri Strip; that now I'm a surgeon.

Eto wobbles on his feet and I grab him before he falls and lie him down, yelling for Imbi to bring some water. I run to the hut and get the first-aid kit and one of the Brazo's T-shirts which I slip over him because he's shivering uncontrollably. Imbi's kneeling beside him, giving him sips of water and talking to him.

I look at his hand. The cut's deep, the blood glossy and slick down his arm.

I empty two vials of saline over it and the crimson flesh is exposed, crossed by the white fibre of a tendon. I dab at it with gauze and it's a relief to realise that it's hardly bleeding, but I get Imbi to sit beside me and mop up any blood that seeps out until I'm ready. Eto stares off into the jungle. He's quiet, concentrating on overcoming the pain, and it blows me away how much he can take as I paw away at the injury. I'd be screaming.

He doesn't flinch as I inject some anaesthetic. I have no idea how much to give him, but I jab the needle in at half a dozen places and squeeze a bit into each.

There are some rubber gloves and I pull them on but it's hard to grip the sutures so I take them off again. Eto spots the needle in my hand and his eyes go wide but I know he trusts me, and he turns back to the jungle.

I poke at his hand a few times with the needle to see if the anaesthetic's worked. Imbi watches, wide-eyed. I know the word for pain and I say it to him and Imbi says something else and he pats my knee and I'm ready to go.

I take a deep breath and blow it out hard, which probably scares the shit out of Eto but he doesn't move and I start stitching. I bring it all together from one end and my knots are a dog's breakfast but I think they'll hold. I put in fourteen stitches in all, and Imbi mops and wipes the blood that oozes out as I go.

I can see that it's an awful job, but I've closed it up well enough and I know it will heal. Imbi looks at me and at the first-aid kit in astonishment, as do all the village women, who've gathered around. It takes a bit of explaining, but finally I get Eto to swallow some antibiotics.

It's then that the rest of the men come back into the clearing, and Joro's first. He comes straight up to have a look and I see his eyes go wide in disbelief and I know then that he's a bit freaked. The wound he inflicted half an hour ago is a wound no more. It must be like seeing a miracle of healing. While he stands there I explain loudly in English to the village that this was the act of a fuckwit, and because I've taught Eto the word he laughs out loud. Joro knows well that I'm taking the piss out of him and I can see him fuming, but Eda's arrived back in the clearing and I can see he's well fucked off with Joro. He sends the village scuttling with a bark and comes to look at Eto's hand. He can't believe it. He watches as I smear some Betadine over the wound and then some of Imbi's paste. Only when I dress it and cover it with a bandage does he go back to his hut.

The next morning, I present Eda with the fishing hooks that I spent the previous day making. I've fashioned two of them from the prongs of the fork I found in the ship, sharpening them on rocks and then bending them and binding them with copper wire and suture twine to the finest woven rope that Imbi could make for me. They won't hold a huge fish, but they take all the force I can put on them with my fingers.

I bent the handle of the fork until it broke in half and then ground it on a rock until it shone. I've lashed that above the hook to act as a sinker, and hopefully the silver flash will attract fish.

I hold them up and say the word for fish to Eda, but he doesn't understand so I get Imbi to tell him that I want to go fishing with him today. He nods and after breakfast we set off.

Eda puts me in his canoe with Eto and a quiet, older man called Mala, and when we get out past the reef Eda nods at me and I try to make him understand that I need bait; that first they have to catch one fish. I can't explain it to him or Eto so eventually he gives up and laughs and he gives the order to begin fishing as usual.

I can see immediately why there's never enough food for the village. Fishing is a waiting game. Eto is only along for the ride because of his hand, but Eda and Mala stare down into the water, bows drawn, waiting for fish to ghost out from under the raft of branches floating on the surface. Down deep I can see good-sized fish swimming around, but they don't come anywhere near the surface. It's half an hour before they shoot the first one, a slender, silver species like a small barracuda. It's not even a meal for one.

I ask Eda for it, and then I point to his knife. He thinks I want to eat the fish straightaway and he refuses, but I hold up my hook and point again at the fish and he understands and reluctantly gives it to me.

I iki the fish to stop it wriggling, then slice out a chunk from near its tail, hoping like fuck that it will make good bait. Eda suddenly twigs what I'm at when I thread the bait on to the hook, and he and Eto keep up a constant chatter as I lower it over the side.

I feel the fork sinker hit the bottom then pull it up a bit and I don't have to wait long. It's struck almost immediately, and I'm suddenly hanging on to a thrashing fish, trying not to let the rope slip through my fingers.

By some miracle the hook holds, and I land it. It's bright blue, a jewel of a fish, fat and muscular. I have no idea what it is, but Eda's excited and he bounces around like a kid. The fish has swallowed the bait and bent the hook slightly, so I stab it into the timber of the canoe and push it back into shape. I slice out another chunk from the silver fish and rebait the hook and lower it down again and the same thing happens.

Now Eda wants to try, a piece of bait already in his hand. I show him how to push the point of the hook two or three times through the skin of the bait and he nods as he does it, talking to himself.

He lowers the hook and screeches with excitement when a fish strikes. But he gets a monster and hauls on the rope too hard and it straightens out the hook, and I can see that it's ruined when we pull it up.

I give him the other hook and he catches two more fish before that one's gone too. But he's chuffed with the discovery, and he and Eto and Mala hold an animated discussion all the way back to the beach.

We walk to the freighter ship that afternoon and I point to any piece of steel that could conceivably become a hook. We wrench and pull at the steel and smash at it with rocks until we have an armload of assorted scrap which we carry back to the village.

I notice on the way back that Eda is labouring; exhausted from the day's exertions. He stumbles through the forest, getting worse the closer we get to home, and when we get to the village he simply drops his load and walks to his hut and rests until he's called for his evening meal. He's haggard and wrecked, but he looks over the start we've made on the hooks and talks to Mala at length.

Mala proves to be a craftsman, rubbing the steel tirelessly against various chunks of rock he keeps in his hut for the purpose. He shows me the knives he's made, and they're the best in the village, blades evenly ridged and honed, their handles bound intricately with tiny shells threaded on to the fibre. He's also chief bow-maker; he has the honour of making Eda's bows.

Mala knocks out a couple of decent hooks, bigger than those I made with the fork, and much stronger.

We try them again the next day, and this time Joro and his mates don't peel off to their own spot but follow along and watch. Within half an hour we've caught more that they'd normally get all day, and Eda calls a halt, refusing to let Joro try the hooks. Joro complains bitterly, but Eda barks at him and Joro paddles away with a face like thunder.

That evening Joro slaps Imbi across the face. I don't see how it starts but I hear the slap and I look up and see her holding her cheek and Joro standing over her.

Eto grabs my arm before I can do anything and tells me to wait. Joro stands over Imbi for a while, but she doesn't meet his gaze and eventually he walks away, muttering to himself. Imbi then gets up and walks to Eda's hut and Eto follows, and I can see them talking to Eda through the door. Eto then calmly walks around to all the other huts, quietly talking to everyone.

Ten minutes later, all of the men in the village gather in the clearing to give Joro a beating. He stands by the fire, waiting for it. He stares directly at me. He's still looking at me when he takes the first punch to the side of his head. They pummel him until he's lying in a heap on the ground. Eda doesn't even come out of his hut.

When Joro recovers enough to get to his feet, he looks again at me and grins, blood glistening from his teeth, before he stalks off into the darkness.

Chapter 21

When Imbi comes to my hut before dawn the next day I can feel when she kisses me that her lip is still swollen where Joro hit her. I start to mention his name but she puts her hand over my lips to shut me up. She kisses me all over, working her way down my body, murmuring something I don't understand. Then I'm away, lost in a dream.

She's possessed with a powerful need when she comes back up to kiss me and we fuck with pressing urgency. She moans, but I no longer care about the noise we make; it's a common enough sound from the huts, and I know now that everyone in the village knows about Imbi and me.

Afterwards, in the deep silence, Imbi falls asleep on my chest. I lie awake, watching the light of dawn grow outside, and I think of home.

Eda is sick as a dog that morning; it's all he can do to grovel to the door of his hut to spew out of it. There are anti-nausea tablets in the first-aid kit and I try to give them to him but he waves me away. I tell Imbi to keep giving him sips of water and by the middle of the day he's recovered a bit. He gets up and walks around the village for a while and then goes back to his hut and sleeps all afternoon and through the night. When I go to check on him the next morning he's up and ready to go fishing.

Mala has upped his game. When we got back from fishing yesterday, I drew a picture on the ground of a hook with a barb and mimed a fish unable to get off it, and Mala nodded enthusiastically but I wasn't sure if he understood what I was saying. I don't know how he did it, but the hook that Eda holds up to me now has a perfect little barb, peeled back from the steel like the skin from a banana. Later I have to use the scalpel to remove that same barb from Eda's finger, but he's unfazed, overjoyed at the day's catch. He even tries some fish cooked over the fire to amuse me but spits it out into the jungle while the rest of the village laughs uproariously at him. There's the air of a party that night: there's so much to eat that we can't finish it. After the meal, the men drum out a beat on logs and the youths dance around the fire. Eda sits beside me and laughs and claps me on the thigh whenever I speak to him.

But by the next morning he's spewing again. This time it's not as bad, and he gets himself together and leaves the village with the rest of the men, but I'm worried. I don't have a clue how to help him. That evening he's bad, and he eats nothing, crawling into his hut without a word. It's a pattern that continues, days stretching to weeks. Some days he bounces back, declaring himself to be healed, but others he can barely peel himself off the floor of his hut, his eyes glazed over with pain and sickness.

I take to sitting in the entrance to his hut and talking to him on the days he's too ill to go fishing, but well enough to sit up and take some food and water. Imbi and Baka often join us, and we spend hours trying to decipher each other. I tell them about my mother, my sister and her daughters. Even if I could figure out some way to explain it, I decide to tell them nothing about modern life; I don't tell them about cars, about high-rise buildings, about ovens and phones. I wouldn't know where to start and I know it would only confuse them if I tried.

I ask them the name of their island; I know it isn't North Sentinel. They don't understand me. I point at myself. "Jimmy," I say. I point at the ground. "Lem?" I ask. Name? They look at each other, lost.

Eda's fond of long diatribes, and through Imbi's patient explanations, I come to understand that Eda is from an unbroken line of leaders of the village for as far back as anyone remembers. They don't understand me when I ask if they know when the people first came to this island – Eda says they have been here forever.

Baka is Eda's only son. None of his other women have borne him any children. He tells me that if Baka had died that day I rescued him, then his reign as chief would have been over. He explains that because Imbi gave him Baka she is now the most important woman in the village and she can choose any man and she chose me. He chuckles when he tells me that I stole Baka back from Biyase, and that Imbi is my prize.

Eda and Imbi keep talking about Biyase and the 'big sea' and it takes me a long time to twig that they're talking about the Boxing Day tsunami in 2004. I get the story out of them slowly, and by using handfuls of shells I learn that they lost more than two hundred people and I'm gobsmacked by it. Eda was fishing when it struck, and he was washed back to the island and through the trees. He shows me the scar where he tore open his leg and tells me that he saw the sun rise twice before they found him. Imbi climbed a tree far inland to escape the waters. She explains that the last medicine person in the village was killed that day, his children along with him.

Eda continues to get worse. I get him to take some painkillers but I'm at a loss as to how else to help him. He has to be helped to the toilet and Imbi tells me that there's blood in his shit, but he's as tough as leather and he rallies some days long enough to sit by the fire and talk to the men in the village.

Eda ignores it, but I can see Joro watching him with malicious interest. He asks about him as soon as he gets back to the village each day, and his eyes follow them whenever Imbi helps Eda to move about. Whenever Eda is resting in his hut Joro becomes bolder, snapping and barking orders at the women.

I surf in the mornings, return to check on Eda and surf again in the afternoon if the waves are good. I sense that the season is just starting to wind down and guess it must be the beginning of September. The time between decent swells starts to lengthen, and often the waves are smaller. I surf Mine almost every morning, but I go somewhere else in the afternoon so that I don't run into Joro and his boys coming back from fishing, when he's always in a shitty mood. He's taken over in Eda's absence, dictating where they fish. Eto and Mala have stopped going out with them, and they catch so many fish on the new hooks there's no need.

It's usually Heartstopper or Mum's in the afternoon, but if the swell's any way kooky I'll surf Freakshow, and if it's big I'll walk to Freights. I haven't properly scored Freights since the big day; the wind has been slightly off, or a difference in the swell direction brings down unmakeable sections.

I break one of the Brazo's boards on a solid day at Mine, snapped clean in two by a wave that was going to land on my head, so I bailed and left the board to its wrath. When I came up I saw the nose bobbing and leaping away in the whitewater far inside as it washed across the reef. That afternoon I retrieved my old board from where I abandoned it, browning in the sun, forgotten. Now it's my back-up board and I cursed myself for not taking better care of it.

One afternoon I leave Eda to Imbi, spewing up his guts in awful, retching convulsions and producing lumps of yellow-green bile. It's obvious now that he's not going to get better. I also know that I need to leave before he dies. There'll be no one to stop Joro after Eda's death, and I'm in no doubt that I'll be the first person he comes for.

When I reach the beach I can see that it's kicked since this morning and it's a good six foot at Mine. But there's a touch of east in the swell and I head for Heartstopper. Sure enough it's firing; great lumps lurch out of the sea and hurl themselves at the reef. Each is like a minor miracle; a transformation from amorphous dark water, to sparkling crystalline structure, and then finally to vaporised foam, like a potter producing a work of art from a shapeless lump of clay, and then smashing it on the ground.

I reach the line-up just as the wind drops completely away, and the sudden clarity seems to bring the reef closer, a florid carpet flowing to and fro beneath my feet. It's both dreamy and intimidating.

It's a classic session; one I'll never forget. When I catch them just right, there's a kind of pause after the take-off, a pregnant potential energy that's released the instant the lip strikes the flat water, cracking like cannon fire. Then it's all on. By the end I'm taking off behind the peak and backdooring great, glossy tongues of water, casually standing tall through the tube from beginning to end. I lose count of my barrels. I feel like a god.

I'm done in when I see the shark. I've been out for four hours or so, and for the last hour I've been trapped in the limbo that I've become used to; thinking that it's less exhausting to turn around and head back out for another one than face the long paddle back to shore. My arms are jelly and I've been waiting for the inevitable cartwheel down the face.

The first thing that goes through my head is a calculation of its size; the shark is fucking big. I can see its dorsal fin and the tip of its tail, and there's at least three metres between them. It's travelling seaward, heading out through the pass, and I don't fully start to freak until it lazily turns and comes my way.

I'm out the back and I immediately lie down and thrash like a madman for a small wave which passes underneath me. To my horror there's nothing behind it, so I keep going, heading straight in, to the reef. It's a fucking stupid thing to do, but I'm panicking, and my only thought is to get away from the shark. I try to calm down, to paddle smoothly, sliding my fingers into the water, but there's no way I'm going to go slowly.

I'm in the worst possible place when the next set arrives but I don't care because its waist-deep and I can stand on the reef. The wave explodes and whitewater roars into me, and I'm tumbled a long way across the reef before I open up my heel on a coral head. The next wave hits and I try to stay flat and swim through it, and then a third pushes me off the back of the reef into deep water, and hard as I try, I can't paddle back to it against the incoming tide and the wash.

I look around wildly but I can't see the shark and it's only then that I go underwater and I spot the huge grey shape sliding beneath me.

I fight every instinct to get back on my board and paddle. I stay vertical in the water and keep my head under until I'm gasping, then I get a quick breath and go under again. I try to keep my eye on the shark as it cruises the reef. It's zigzagging, swimming away from me and then coming back in, each time getting a little closer. When it starts to swim more quickly, I really shit myself. I can see the hazy pink blush of blood around my heel and I try to cover the wound with my hand but it makes it hard to turn and follow the shark and I let it go again.

The shark starts making little speed runs at me, turning away at the last second, and I can see the stripes on its side and its great black eye as it passes. I recoil from it each time, trying to swim backwards and screaming underwater. After each pass I take a breath, but no sooner do I go under again than I'm bursting for another one.

I lose it in the gloom but seconds later it reappears and comes straight for me and I make up my mind to have a go at it. This time when it comes at me I force myself to punch at it before it turns away, and I land the feeblest of prods on its nose. But it reacts immediately, flashing away at shocking speed, its slashing tail ripping at the surface, turning it to foam.

I keep coming up and going under, gasping for breath, and it keeps slicing towards me, and I manage to pop it once more before I finally see it turn and swim away. I stay under, watching for it as I swim backwards towards a bridge of reef that goes all the way to shore, and I don't relax until I'm standing in ankle-deep water. I shout like a lunatic with the relief of it. It takes me half an hour to hobble across the coral to the beach, but there's no way I'm getting back in the water. When I reach the sand, it's getting dark. I lie down and close my eyes until the adrenaline has gone from my body, but the sense of dread remains.

Chapter 22

Well before dawn Imbi climbs into my hut and tells me that Eda's not going to last much longer. I go to get up to check on him, but she stops me, saying that two of the other women are there with him.

In the evening I tried to get him to take some Tramadol, the strongest painkiller I have in the kit, but he was unable to swallow it. He was wracked with cramps and shivering, a sheen of sweat over his body. Imbi and I could do nothing but give him water and keep him company, but he was ranting; half in and out of consciousness. Imbi said he was talking to Biyase.

Imbi's quiet, lying on her back, and I kiss her and tell her I'm sorry. She says nothing, and I know she's thinking about what the future holds. I know she's worried about me. She rolls towards me and we lie on our sides, our faces together, her breath sweet and herbal. When I kiss her neck, she rolls on top of me and moans when I breathe in her ears and then take her nipple in my mouth.

I hold her hips as we fuck slowly, but our desire gets the better of us and then it's headlong and heedless. She's insatiable, trying to get me deeper inside her, gyrating and grinding until she gasps and collapses on top of me.

When Imbi lies down beside me she falls asleep almost immediately. I listen to her breathing in the darkness. I know that she's in danger, and so is Baka. Joro will probably kill Eto and Mala too. But as I lie there feeling Imbi's breath on my skin I tell myself that it's none of my business.

I see a crack of light through the walls. It's almost dawn. Sitting up, I reach up into the rafters and grab the bundled-up boardies and the Brazos' T-shirts and the surf hat. I've stashed six tubes of water, sealing them with suture twine, and I put them under my arm and slip out of the hut. A hiss from the embers of last night's fire is the only sound I hear when I pass through the clearing and step into the jungle, making for the beach.

I taste the salt spray and hear the static, rushing roar of the ocean long before I step out of the trees on to the beach. I gasp as I catch sight of the reef. The pass is a pass no more; giant, cresting walls break right through the centre of it, closing out the entire bay. Thigh-high waves muscle themselves on to the shore at my feet, their energy enduring across the entire lagoon. I stare at the maelstrom on the reef for a long time, speechless. I won't be leaving today.

My scalp prickles and I glance back at the jungle. My mind is suddenly thick with panic. I'm convinced that Joro is about to explode out of the trees, his bow raised.

Looking down at the clothes and water in my hands, I realise that I have to get rid of them before anyone sees, and I stash them all in the jungle beside the outboard motor and petrol tanks and pull the palms back over it all. Then I return to the beach and sit on the sand, forcing myself to take deep breaths until I calm down a bit.

I stare out at the reef and I know I'm getting my shit together when I start to analyse the conditions. The softest of south-east breezes ruffles the towering ridgeline of each gigantic wave, but it's a clean groundswell and I count eighteen seconds between waves.

I tuck the Brazo's surfboard under my arm and set off down the track to Freights. I have to see if it's working, but my thoughts are fractured and fleeting as I walk through the jungle. I'm unable to concentrate, unable to process the danger I know I'm in. Fear comes upon me in pulses, and just as rapidly my panicked brain gallops away from it. Images of the two boys curled in their sandy graves flash through my mind. I'm on autopilot when I emerge from the trees to get my first look at Freights.

The rising sun has found space between the horizon and a bank of low cloud, turning the sky mauve, the ocean indigo. Giant, tapering walls scream their way across the reef at Freights, and I can see immediately that it's flawless; each wave a rhythmic, frictionless procession along the point.

I'm still a hundred metres away, paddling out, when I get a true sense of the size of the surf. The faces are fifteen to twenty feet. At the end of the point they thunder out into the channel and subside into the deep, and I'm even intimidated by what's left over; I can feel their power as the hulking lumps slide beneath me. I'm out of my league by an order of magnitude entirely unfamiliar to me. I know I should turn around and head back in, but I'm mesmerised and I keep going. I need to get a closer look.

I stop halfway up the point and sit and watch, transfixed, at every wave that steams past. They're each a phenomenon, an event all of their own. At Snapper, on the big, ruler-edged days where the local chargers fearlessly pull into the yawning sandy pits behind the rock, I've often found myself looking back at shore, at the people walking around, the cars on the roads, and thought, 'don't you know what's happening out here?'

They're like sheep, automatons, buying coffee and staring at their phones, while at sea things of great importance are taking place; gladiators are doing battle, and those feats of skill and bravery deserve a slack-jawed audience, lining the shore to watch.

Without conscious thought I find myself at the top of the reef. The sight of each oncoming swell, lifting itself out of the ocean beyond the take-off point, seems to defy logic. They emerge, giant creatures from the deep, and further along the reef to the south they start to feather and cap, but it's clear where the wave truly begins.

I can see that Freights was made for this size; it doesn't break wide, no matter how big the wave – the playing field is almost as tight as any other day I've surfed here. At six foot there's a wrinkle, an imperfection in the take-off, but at this size there's no sign of it. The reef has ironed it out, moulding each wave perfectly, their concave ramps flawless, as though designed by an engineer.

Because I have no immediate plan to surf these waves, I actually appreciate the beauty of what I'm seeing. I stare down into the sepulchral depths of each one, mesmerised by the cave being created before my eyes. But when the lip completes the circle and cracks off the water with a sound like a cannon firing, I'm jerked from my reverie. It's the beginning of a prolonged explosion, a chain reaction of detonations down the reef. The whitewater, too, is like nothing I've ever seen. It looks like the towering head of an avalanche, boiling and leaping and roaring across the surface of the sea in a furious tumult.

I sit and watch for twenty minutes and a familiar feeling builds. I'm paralysed with terror, and then filled with disgust for myself. I'm afraid out here, and I'm afraid on the island. I've always been afraid. My fear, my cowardice, follows me everywhere – even here, to the ends of the earth.

If there was a bottle of whiskey on the beach I'd paddle in and drink it as fast as I could, for dangerous and self-destructive oblivion. But instead I have a tiny surfboard and waves like buildings and it seems like an appropriate alternative for the impulse to self-harm that grips me now. I find myself padding into the take-off zone, reckless abandon flip-flopping wildly with cold terror.

As luck would have it, the first wave that rears is the largest I've seen so far. I scratch for the horizon and I'm surprised when I clear it easily, but looking down, I can see why; the reef drops sharply away, disappearing into the deep blue. It's the source of the wave's power, the compressive mechanism, the reason the swell magnifies so spectacularly. I turn and paddle back in again for the second wave, possessed with a heedless abandon, but it passes beneath me like a nuclear submarine.

There's a third wave in the set, and I can't believe I'm paddling for it, but my mind seems to be disregarding any instinct for survival. I hear my own breathing, fast and ragged, and I feel as though I'm in a dream when the wave rears behind me. I don't even look back; just put my head down and go. I rise and rise, backsliding up the face until it seems an impossibility that the wave can actually be caught, but then there's a sudden reversal and I'm bulldozed forward at a speed that I can barely credit. Rigid with fear, I manage to scramble to my feet and assume a survival stance as I take the drop. It goes on forever and there's too much speed to even contemplate a bottom turn and when I hear the wave detonate behind me I know that I'm lost. I hold my course, trying to stay ahead of the whitewater, but it explodes into my back. I'm blown clean off the board and then there's nothing but violence, terrifying and brutal and never-ending. It's the worst beating I've ever had, but incredibly I don't hit the reef and for the first fifteen seconds or so I'm strangely calm. I seem to be observing myself. But when it doesn't let me go a panic grips and I slash at the aerated water. I claw and kick for a long time before I burst through and get a breath. Looking seaward, I see that there aren't any more waves in the set. I'm surprised to see that my board's still at the end of my leggie. I haul it in and sprint for the channel.

By the time I get to safety I've already decided to try again. I spend another half an hour watching it, trying to figure out the best approach. I was too far out on the shoulder, I realise, and it brings a lump to my throat knowing that I have to paddle deeper, to go further inside.

I play a trick on myself. I tell myself that I can ride one of these waves, and I repeat it over and over, managing to hold on to that conviction until I'm back in the line-up. I let three more sets pass, waiting for the one that peaks further inside. I have to overcome a base terror to paddle deeper, and I'm still not where I should be; every cell in my body screams at me to sit on the shoulder. But when I crest a smaller wave and then see the one that I've been looking for, I stroke in fast and deep and get there in time.

Again, the endless backslide up the face, but there's more calculation in my movements this time. When the shunt comes I'm ready for it and I'm on my feet early and immediately I see that I've given myself more time. I get my toes on the rail and set an angle down the face, and as it starts to heave I'm suddenly charged with its power. The acceleration is breathtaking, exponential. By the time I reach the bottom my board seems not to touch the wave at all.

This time I manage a bottom turn, but even so I've skittered too far out on the flats again. When I look down the line the sight is horrifying; a wall the size of a prison's, stretching so far in front of me it looks like it belongs to another wave entirely.

I brace for the crushing impact of the lip as I haul the board around, not daring to look anywhere but down the line. Behind me comes the appalling thunderclap.

I make it around the cascading lip. I'm so stunned that I almost blow it immediately, rising too high up the face. The wall steepens frighteningly quickly, and I'm almost back where I started, faced with negotiating another heart-stopping drop.

I cling on by my toenails, willing myself not to go up and over, and angle down. It has the effect of generating yet more speed, and when finally I set a decent line I'm supersonic.

But so is the wave. I would have been happy to ride out its length as far ahead of the barrel as possible, but it won't be an option. The wall is rearing far ahead and there's nothing more I can do. A slab of water like the side of a two-storey house stands vertical in front of me, and then folds itself over.

The future is forgotten, replaced by the immediacy of what's happening under my feet, above me. I'm inside the cathedral of its yawning belly. All is white noise and hissing spray, matching what's going on in my head. I've become unthinking, elemental. Something releases in my muscles; my knees bend, my shoulders drop, my feet flex and make minute adjustments to my board. I'm barely aware of it; my movements are muscle memory, involuntary. Every wave I've ever caught has led up to this moment. My fear is gone.

I fly through the cavernous tunnel for a long time. Ahead, the wall keeps looming, throwing, looming, throwing. The wave is omnipotent, all-powerful. Just as it seems like it will go on forever, it comes to an end. I can't see a thing in the final spit of the wave, and I close my eyes, and it's only when I'm skimming out into the channel that it clears and I can see again. I turn and look behind me and it's like a magic trick; it seems implausible that the wave is no more, replaced by a glittering sheen of foam across the surface of the sea.

Chapter 23

When I get back to the village, Eda's dead. He's laid out in the middle of the clearing. The earth around him has been swept clean; fine lines made by branches radiate out from him to the edge of the forest, like he's the centre of a sun. The Sentinelese sit around him in a circle, women on one side and the men on the other. The children sit in front of their mothers.

I slip in beside Eto and no one looks at me except for Baka, who gives me a smile which I try to return, but I'm sick with dread for him.

Imbi runs proceedings, talking for a long time. I understand some of it; she talks of what Eda has seen; the ocean, fish, the earth, birds and insects, Biyase. She talks about Baka. When she's finished, she nods to him and the boy rises and goes to his father and places two shells over his eyes. Baka looks at Imbi for approval and she smiles at him. Then, one by one, every member of the village goes up to Eda and, on their hands and knees, whisper in each of his ears. Imbi tells me later that night that in one ear they told him their secrets, and in the other their hopes. He takes their secrets to his grave and asks Biyase to grant their hopes. She also says that it's Biyase's last task; then he is no more, Eda is their new god, and it's only then I twig that Biyase was Eda's father, the chief before him.

When every person in the village has whispered into Eda's ears, they mix water and dirt and plug the mud into his ears. Lastly, his mouth is filled with food; dried fish, fruits, vegetables until it gapes open. Then the men pick him up and walk away with him on their shoulders, to bury him in the jungle.

When the men return there's a meal, then the whole village gathers around the fire where each person has the chance to speak about Eda. Even the smallest children talk, granted absolute silence by the rest of the village. The competition seems to be who can tell the funniest story, and by the end men and women are howling with laughter, rolling on the ground. It could be the aftermatch of any good funeral, and watching them all crack up like that makes me miss my mum and sister and my mates. It's made even better because Joro isn't there; I saw him walk off into the jungle in the direction of the beach immediately after dinner.

I know I have to leave as soon as I can or Joro and his boys will kill me, and I'm frightened that they'll try it tonight. But Joro's mates are here around the fire, while he isn't, so planning for my death is either completed or not yet done. I'm fairly sure that Joro, evil fucker that he is, won't hurry to kill me; he'll draw it out, but still I can't see myself lasting all of tomorrow. It gives me the shits thinking of trying to get through the pass if the swell is still macking.

In my hut with Imbi that night I don't say anything, but the light of the dying fire comes through the cracks to pick out the glint of a tear on her cheek and I'm pretty sure she knows what I'm planning. She can see that the boardies, hat and T-shirts are gone from the rafters; she saw the water tubes. She lies on my chest, murmuring softly to me.

But to my surprise it's Imbi who wakes me in the pitch-black morning. She puts her hand over my mouth and pulls me towards the entrance of the hut where she crouches, listening. I come to the entrance and Imbi slips out, pulling me after her. I don't know if she's heard something, but the village is as still as a stone as far as I can see in the darkness.

Imbi guides me through the clearing and into the jungle, but we've only gone a little way when she tells me to wait and jogs back to the clearing. I can just see her through the trees as she creeps to the entrance of Joro's hut and my hair stands on end at the sight of it. She crouches down outside his hut and then she straightens and turns and walks to the fire where I see a little puff of orange sparks rise up as she drops something into the embers.

I ask her what it was when she reaches me, and she tells me it was Joro's bow, and it's then that I know she's helping me to escape. I kiss her and wrap her into a hug, but inside I'm a scurrying rat and it burns up into my throat as I stumble through the jungle after her.

It's so dark that it takes a long time to get to the beach but coming out of the trees I can see a blush of light on the horizon. It's enough to see that the swell has died away to little more than head height; it seems hard to credit that something possessed of that much power could simply disappear. The pass sits as calm and unruffled as ever.

Imbi doesn't look surprised when I pull the branches away from the outboard motor and the petrol tanks. She carries one of the tanks to the beach as I drag the outboard through the trees onto the beach and around to the transom of the Brazos' boat.

When my foot brushes the adze lying in the sand, I know that something is wrong. I look into the boat in the dim light and I can see the holes smashed all through the bottom of it. Joro's done a thorough job, splintering ribs and piercing holes from bow to stern.

My heart starts to pound in my chest as I peer into the inky blackness of the jungle. I drop the outboard on the sand and pick up the adze and stand there for a moment, watching the trees.

Imbi doesn't say a word. She just runs back up the beach, calling me to her, and when I catch up she's already hauling desperately on an outrigger canoe, hissing at me to help. We drag it down the sand and into the water and she runs back into the trees and comes back with two paddles, and for a moment I think she wants to come with me. But she puts one into the bottom of the canoe and hands the other to me and then she crushes herself to me. Her cheeks are wet with tears and I try to kiss her, but she pushes me away and I get into the canoe and she shoves me off.

I paddle a few strokes and turn, then a few more and turn again. She's frantic that I go, that I hurry, but I'm struggling to abandon her. I'm a fucking coward and she knows it, because she doesn't ask anything of me, she doesn't want me to stay and protect her and Baka. I turn and paddle towards the pass without looking back, tears streaming down my face and a cold stone in my chest.

I'm halfway out to the pass when I realise that I've forgotten the water and the clothing, and I stop and turn the canoe around and start to paddle back in. I can see Imbi, still standing on the beach, and then I see a man come out of the jungle behind her and I know that it's Joro.

I scream a warning to her, and she turns, but Joro's too quick and he clocks her, and I see her go down in the sand. Then Joro's into the trees and re-emerging with a canoe, hauling it across the beach. Imbi gets to her feet and I can hear her voice across the water screaming for me to go, and I think Joro's going to hit her again, but he only has eyes for me. He slides the canoe into the water, leaps in and starts paddling.

I spin the canoe around again, and paddle like fuck for the pass. I think of the adze back on the beach as I go, because I know that Joro will have his knife at least.

My arms are already burning by the time I get through the pass and turn east around the finger of the reef. I glance back and see that Joro's made some ground on me, closing the gap to just three hundred metres between us.

I try to settle into a rhythm, to regulate my breathing, to make my strokes more efficient. Now that I'm not thrashing at the water, the canoe glides easily over the glassy humps of swell sliding beneath it. The burn in my arms doesn't back off, but it's manageable.

Joro keeps up his furious pace for another while and comes within two hundred metres, but then I seem to have his measure. We paddle for a long time – ten minutes stretches to half an hour, then one, then two – with the same distance between us, the island now a thin shadow far behind. But sweat is pouring off me and I'm just about done in.

A towering thunderhead opens up and it begins to pelt rain. It revives me a bit and when it puddles in the bottom of the canoe, I stop paddling for a few seconds to try to suck some of it up. Then I put in a prolonged burst, hoping that Joro will give up. But the fucker keeps going. My fear is a constant, electrostatic hum, and the adrenaline it keeps pumping around my body is taking its toll.

I hit a wall. My heart jacks up and up, pounding wildly, a pulsing rush in my ears. A wave of nausea comes over me and I feel suddenly sluggish, my arms like jelly. I panic and keep paddling, but I've lost all power, and my strokes are as feeble as a child's.

The fear prickles across my scalp, streaks up and down my spine. I glance behind, expecting to see Joro steaming up on me, but I'm shocked to see he's actually lost some ground and I almost cry out with relief. I keep going, turning as I paddle, taking quick looks at him, and he's getting nowhere. But I feel awful, like my heart's going to explode. My breathing is ragged, rasping out of my throat. Somehow, I paddle for another ten minutes, and when I next turn around Joro has stopped. I stop too. It feels so fucking good to stop paddling.

The rain is turning the sea to stippled foam, the droplets generating a sibilant white noise on the water. I peer through it. He's too far away to see the look on his face, but I see that he's standing up in his canoe, facing my way.

The relief of not having to paddle any more washes across me and I greedily suck the rain from the gunwales and the bottom of the canoe. I drink like an antelope at a watering hole, watching for the lion, dropping my head and drinking and then raising it again quickly. But Joro doesn't come for me.

The rain stops as quickly as it began. The wall recedes, and I feel renewed, energised by the water in my belly. I wait for Joro to begin after me again. I can see him clearly now and his canoe has drifted side-on to me. He stares at me silently, still standing, but as I watch he sits again and takes up his paddle. I get ready to go, but instead he turns his canoe back for North Sentinel and starts to paddle home.

For a minute or so I do nothing, just sit quietly in the canoe watching Joro get further away. The realisation that I'm safe washes over me in progressive waves; my lizard brain, focused by fear, now expands. I think of home.

I think of my sister and the girls, of Jess, of Willo and the boys, and then I think of my mum.

My dad bullies his way in, and a memory comes to me like a hammer blow across the head.

"Fuck off out of it you little arsehole," he says to me as he passes. I see every freckle and hair on his back as he goes into their bedroom and closes the door behind him. Then I hear the muffled thumps, the slaps, the frightened yelps from Mum. I'm sitting in the hallway, rigid, rocking, doing nothing, and then Rachel comes in from outside, the skinny strip of her, and hears the noises and tears past me, barging into their room and screaming so ferociously that Dad stops. He actually fucking stops. She keeps screaming at him, right into his face until he smacks her one, too, but she stands up again and keeps going, and I can't believe it when he comes tearing past me and fucks off outside.

At some point after that my trauma was replaced by shame, and it sticks to me like shit to a shoe.

Joro's a good six hundred metres away when I whistle to him. He doesn't hear me, so I go again and then I see him stop paddling and turn around. I start towards him, my knuckles white around the shaft of the paddle, my throat tightening.

Joro spins his canoe around and paddles slowly towards me. My hair stands on end. I reckon he thinks I'm going to tease him and turn away again, but as we get closer to each other and I don't deviate from the course, I see him start to dig it in.

I try to keep my pace slow, my breathing deep. I'm trying to think, to plan. I know there won't be much opportunity.

It takes less than three minutes for the two canoes to reach each other. Joro's smoking along, breathing hard, the ropes of muscle in his arms slick with rainwater and sweat, his eyes wide with furious bloodlust.

Suddenly there's only ten metres between us. Joro stops paddling and pulls out his knife, and it's then that I finally paddle hard, driving my canoe forward with everything I've got.

As I'd hoped, Joro gets to his feet and moves to the front of his canoe, his knife held up, ready to sink into me. I give it two more strokes, rise to my hunkers and, as I ram into his outrigger, I jump at him. His canoe skews wildly under the impact and he's off balance when I smack into him, but I feel the knife plunge into the flesh around my collarbone. Then he draws it back again for another go. But we're tumbling off the canoe and into the sea and I know that this is my chance.

I get a hold of his knife hand and manage to clamp it under my arm. He bends it at the wrist and the knife pierces my side but I don't feel much pain. I kick like mad, down as deep as I can, until we're well below the surface. He thrashes at me with his free hand for a moment, but then he's trying to swim with it, to pull himself to the surface. I wrap my legs around his to stop him kicking, and his one arm isn't enough to bring both of us back up.

I try to relax, to take myself to the place a big-wave wipeout demands that a surfer go in the midst of his fear. Joro struggles like a frenzied kingfish, thrashing against me, but I keep hold. I can feel his knife slicing a crosshatch of cuts into my side, but his arm's too far through to drive it in deep, and not far enough to bend it to do the same.

It seems to go on forever, but then gradually his struggles weaken, and then cease. The knife stops its scratching. I think of Imbi. Still I stay under, my diaphragm spasming with the need for air, but my mind without desire for it, a dangerous quiescence coming over me. The pop and fizz of the ocean lulls me. Then, I open up my arms and legs wide and Joro drifts away from me, his hands hanging from outstretched arms like a scarecrow's.

It's only when my view of him is obscured by the maroon mist of the blood coming from my wounds that I'm snapped from my trance, and it comes as a shock when I break the surface at how weak I am, how close to passing out. It's all I can do to swim to my canoe and hang on to the bow until my breath restores my strength.

It takes me a long time to haul myself into the canoe. I lie down, done-in, my head over the gunwale. As though in a dream I study the dark shape of Joro's body suspended in the water column below me. The wind has died away completely, and the only audible sound is that of droplets of water and blood from my hair and collarbone striking the surface of the sea.

Chapter 24

I didn't make it back to Port Blair, at least not under my own steam. They told me that when the fishing boat found me, I was about halfway there. They said that I was lying on my back in the bottom of the canoe, stark-naked, blood congealing in dark, greasy lumps across my chest. They said that my eyes were open, and the fishermen thought I was dead until they got close enough to see that my chest was moving. Of my rescue I only remember the vague shouts of men, strong hands moving me about, the smell of cigarettes and the throb of an engine. Then there's nothing until I woke between the sheets of a hospital bed in Port Blair.

I'm on the plane now, an Emirates flight from Kolkata to Brisbane that my sister had to pay for because all my stuff in the hotel was long gone. The ice in my drink stings my teeth, and the air conditioning makes me shiver.

They're going to get a shock when they see me. I'm thin; when I went to do up my seatbelt, I had to tighten it to child proportions.

My hair and beard are bleached, long and wild. My face is peeling from sunburn. The women beside me looks like she's going to strike up a conversation but thinks the better of it.

The smog was soup-like out of Kolkata, but as we head out over the Bay of Bengal it clears to reveal the cerulean expanse of the Indian Ocean. I sit, my forehead resting against the window, searching the endless blue for the jade dot of North Sentinel Island. I check the route we're flying on the plane's flight information screen, and it looks as though we're going to pass right over it. I spot the other islands in the archipelago, but North Sentinel must be directly below us and I can't catch sight of it no matter how I crane my neck. I imagine Imbi and Baka looking up, pointing at the vapour trail in the sky. Then, the islands drift away behind us, and there's nothing but the blue of the Andaman Sea.

I push the bell, and when the stewardess comes I ask for another drink. Then, I choose a movie and plug in my headphones.

Author's note:

I'm a lot like Jimmy. I'll do almost anything to avoid the crowds, to find a spot to surf alone or with just a few mates. When it (occasionally) happens, when that hustle is removed, leaving just the pure experience, it's truly the best thing in the world. In fact, I love that experience so much that I've written a book about it, and there's a certain satisfaction in living vicariously through Jimmy and playing out this fantasy on the page.

However, there is one thing that I think is important to say. This is a work of fiction. I have never been to North Sentinel Island, and I will never go.

I've put this note at the back of this book, rather than the front, so that you could suspend disbelief and imagine what it would be like to discover an island chock-full of world-class waves and have it all to yourself, like an early surf pioneer.

I first became aware of North Sentinel Island when the American missionary, John Chau, visited the island in 2018 and was immediately killed by the Sentinelese. It seemed incredible to me that no outsiders have ever visited the island and lived to tell the tale. I thought it would make the perfect setting for a book since no one knows a thing about the language, culture and customs of the Sentinelese. Needless to say, everything

I wrote about that is fiction, too. I mean no disrespect by it, and I'm comforted by the fact that no Sentinelese person will ever read it.

In all reality I have no idea what the waves there are like. They're probably terrible. It goes without saying, but since people often have a habit of doing crazy stuff, I'll say it anyway: please don't go there!

I really hope you enjoyed the book! Thanks so much for choosing it.

Please do take the time to rate the book or write a review on Amazon – just a few lines would much appreciated!

Sign up

Building a relationship with my readers is important to me. Sign up for my newsletter about upcoming books and added free extras exclusive to my readers at **www.dragonbrothersbooks.com/saltnewsletter**

Also, by James Russell

Coming August 1, 2021

*I'm sitting right in the spot. I couldn't be better positioned.
I know he'll be disgusted if I let the wave pass. The thought of it
wrestles with my fear, then overcomes it, and with my heart in my
mouth I put my head down and go.*

When Sam travels to the west coast of Ireland, he's irresistibly
drawn to the beauty of the landscape, the wildness of the surf,
and the charismatic madness of the locals.

But when he finds himself broke and desperate, and the
opportunity arises to make an illegal quick buck, he takes it.
It starts an unstoppable ripple effect with consequences more
deadly than he ever could have imagined.

Chapter 1

When Anto picks me up it's still dark. As usual he bashes on my window and yells, making enough noise to wake the neighbourhood. I jump out of bed and pull back the curtains to make him stop and he's all mad eyes and teeth through the window. Here's Johnny, he hisses, then gives me the finger and lopes off up the lane into the darkness.

I'm surprised that I didn't hear his Jeep because I was already awake, wondering if he'd come and hoping like fuck he wouldn't. My head's pounding and my mouth is thick with a chemical tang. I pull on some clothes and a puffer jacket, swallow some Panadol and take a long drink from the bathroom tap.

I have to lean hard on front door to open it because the lock is still all bent to shit. Outside, I see Anto's tail lights up the road a bit. The glow from them picks out the squat black beetle of the jetski tethered behind on its trailer and it sends a squirt of apprehension through me. I retch a couple of times, then spit viscous saliva onto the frozen grass. The nausea is replaced with a strange lethargy as I bundle up my wettie, hood, booties and gloves into a towel and grab my board from the shed. I trudge up the lane, the frosty gravel crunching under my shoes.

As I get closer I see Anto sitting on the bonnet. He looks jittery, nervous, scanning up and down the street, even though no one in their right mind is out of the bed at this hour. I'm jittery too – it's an occupational hazard by this point.

He smiles when he sees me coming.

"Morning Sam. You bring the rhino chaser?" he asks, nodding at my board. "Cos it's on!" He grins like a lunatic. As I get close the stale reek of booze reaches me and I get a decent look at him. He's wired; he's obviously pulled an all-nighter.

"How do you know?" I say. "It's pitch dark."

"I can fucking feel it," he hisses, thumping my shoulder.

We take off with Anto's trademark screech of rubber and tear through the streets, the trailer clanking and jouncing behind us.

"I fucking love this car," says Anto.

Getting about through the rural villages of the west of Ireland in this rig makes us stick out like a sore thumb, but there it is. Anto doesn't give a fuck. Dumb culchie boggers, he calls the locals. Hedge-hopping spasos.

We go past Donnaghy's Pub, and both of us stare out at it as we pass. It was less than six hours ago that we'd stumbled out of it onto the silent street, off our faces, and Bren had held high a licked finger and declared that the wind had turned offshore. We'd agreed to surf in the morning.

"That was some craic, last night," says Anto. He's boggling around in his seat, checking the rear-view mirror, then twisting to look behind him. He's manic. He winds up the Jeep out of Bundoran and onto the open road.

"Yeah. Are you still high?" I ask unnecessarily.

"As a fucking kite," he grins. "Bren and me had a few nightcaps."

"Was that wise, Anto?" I ask.

"Sorry, Dad," he replies.

Fifteen minutes later we go past Mullaghmore Harbour and I peer out into the darkness. There's no one around. The headlights illuminate the foam banking up against the stone walls and gathering around the fishing boats like suds in a bathtub; the pulverised remains of the oceanic washing machine agitating out there in the darkness. When we get up onto the head road Anto pulls over, shuts off the engine and winds down his window. A rumble, an energy, like a distant train, bullies its way in, filling the space with more than just sound. Anto's eyes bulge at me.

"It's big, Sam," he says, grabbing my arm. "It's fucking big." He squirms and bounces, peering out into the darkness.

We sit and wait. Anto grows more animated, more hyper, but I retreat into my own head, apprehension gluing together my thoughts, my words. He's talking about later, the Dublin drop, but I've tuned him out.

Finally, Anto can't take it any longer; he jumps out of the Jeep and runs to the edge of the rocks and starts pointing at things I can't see.

A ribbon of grey appears on the horizon behind us. Morning is on its way. I look at my phone, checking for messages, hoping for safety in numbers, someone to talk sense. When Anto comes back to the Jeep he comes around to my side and I wind down the window.

I'll have a Big Mac combo please," he says, hopping from one foot to the other. He pulls off his beanie and his woolly hair springs out like a Brillo pad, adding to the crazy. "There's not a puff of wind. I say we paddle it."

I swallow.

"Fuck Anto… I'm hungover as shit… this is… " I mumble, but tail off lamely. Nothing I say is going to make any difference. His mind is made up. He confirms it.

"You coming or what?"

He doesn't pronounce the 't' in words, does Anto. 'You coming or wha?' Usually I give him shit about it, mimic him, but not today.

"We waiting for the others?"

Anto smiles.

"Nah. Bren isn't coming, that's for sure. He was puking his guts up when I left him."

"What about Mikey?"

Anto shrugs.

"Who knows? Maybe he'll catch up," he says.

Anto flings opens the back of the Jeep and starts rummaging for his wetsuit. I get out, cross the road and sit down on a rock. The air is filled with an electricity, a salt-water charge. The sound booms in the darkness, seems to come from every direction all at once.

Anto's fully suited up by the time dawn starts to illuminate the bay. He sits down beside me, but his legs hammer up and down like sewing machines.

It's only the broad lines of whitewater that can be seen at first, confusedly disassembling themselves on the rocks below us. Kelp whips and thrashes. Then, fifteen minutes later, the surf begins to reveal itself through the growing light. Giant grey slabs rear out of the deep, darkening ominously as they stand up on the reef. More increments of light reveal the cavernous barrels, the walls hauling themselves erect down the line. They seem to fold over in slow motion, an optical illusion created by their sheer size, the way a building seems to slowly crumple after its foundations are dynamited. Anto hops from foot to foot. He pronounces it triple overhead, but just as he does a set looms that re-calibrates his estimate.

"Oh fuck, oh fuck," he says. "Sam. Look at that thing."

We stand and stare as a giant wave turns itself inside out on the reef. The crack and boom of it breaking is like distant thunder; it travels to a place deep inside my gut. The wave pounds its way down the reef, great puffs of spray exploding through the roof, and being vomited from its mouth.

"Did you see how fucking perfect that was?" shouts Anto, but all I saw was the awful maelstrom, the violence.

I go around to the back of the Jeep and pick up my wetsuit, and I see the packages still piled in the back. There's a ragged hole in one of them and I try not to think about it.

My suit's still wet from two days ago and stiff with the cold. By the time I'm into it Anto has hauled out both guns from the board bags and is furiously waxing his.

I try one last time.

"Let's take the ski, Anto."

"Fuck that," he replies, not looking up. "This is our day, Sam."

"I'm out of my league, mate," I try, but Anto's having none of it.

"Bullshit," he replies. "You're better than all of us."

He finally stops waxing and looks up at me.

"I'll go out there on my own, I swear I will. I don't fucking want to, but I will."

I don't say anything, but instead pick up the half block of wax Anto has left on the ground and start to rub it over my board.

Anto dives at me and lands on my back like Gollum in Lord of the Rings. "You little ripper," he mocks in his awful Aussie accent. "You little fucking beauty!"

As we make our way down onto the rocks I start to feel like I'm going to spew, and I don't know if it's the hangover or sheer terror. I hope like fuck there's a crew around at the boat ramp launching skis. Before we locked the Jeep I sent a text to Mikey, but there was no reply.

The surface of the sea is black gloss; not a puff of wind blows in any direction, which is some sort of miracle out here where it's normally blowing forty bastards. Overhead, it looks like the day will be illuminated no further. Clouds like haematomas have arrived to cover the sky. This fucking country, I think, doesn't have the first clue how to do sun. I think of the coast of Western Australia, the endless blue of the ocean and the sky, the light like crystal; hard and delicate all at once.

I know what's coming. It's a long paddle which starts in calm water and finishes twenty minutes later in an environment so violent and frightening my first instinct is always to turn around and paddle straight back in again. This is my third time out here, but never in size like this. We plunge in and paddle hard because the water is so fucking cold. It seeps in through the seams in my wetsuit, bullies its way into my booties and gloves. My board, all nine foot six of it, feels alien – like a tool I don't yet know how to use.

Once we break out of the lagoon and into deep water there's a thick scum which is all that remains of the behemoths expending themselves on the outer reef. Our hair isn't even wet. Even here there's a tonne of water moving, and the speed of the sweep is mad, pushing us further into the bay until we can get well off the rocks and out of the current. Broad-backed swells thirty metres wide pulse below me. I can feel the power of them as they pass; they lift and push me shoreward for an age before passing beneath me, depositing me into the trough.

Halfway out to the top of the point the sun peeps above the horizon and finds space between the hills and the cloud. But there's no rose-coloured glow to the sunrise. Instead, the ocean surface turns silver, like the scales of an enormous fish, and the waves look like collapsing piles of scrap metal. They steam towards us like ocean liners; each an entity of its own, seemingly dispossessed of the sea, and charged with an awful, freakish power. The noise as they break down the line is incredible. We're out far enough now that I begin to spot the boils in front of the waves; they pulse and gush at the surface like geysers, the signs of submarine rocks I don't want to think about. I can't tear my eyes away from the barrel as we paddle towards each wave; a gaping black cave with a concrete mixer churning furiously at the rear.

Anto's thirty metres in front of me, and just as he reaches the crest of a wave, I see him stiffen, pivot his board out into the bay and start hauling arse. He's gone from view when I hear him yelp.

Immediately I turn out to sea, too, even though I can't yet see what's coming. Five seconds later I top the wave he went over, and a looming set is revealed that comes from another realm entirely. The wall of the first wave of the set seems to stretch out across the bay. It's going to close out and take Anto and me with it. It's already feathering, and he's well ahead of me, flat to his board and paddling for all he's worth. Fear rips through me, spurring me on, and I put my head down and paddle at an angle, but I know I'm lost and will end up getting it squarely on the head.

It seems to take forever, paddling across that flat expanse. Somehow Anto makes it over the top of the wave, but it's standing up now, hauling its appalling mass skyward to form a wall like the side of a barn. Deep inside it starts to fold itself over, but I don't look at it – I can't – and as it breaks there's a boom like cannon fire.

Terror dulls my senses. I don't know whether to stop or keep going, but I do the latter, and I get five more strokes in before I realise I'm going to make it; the reef here is so distinct, the channel so deep, that the wave doesn't close out after all, but screams across the reef with a terrifying precision.

The next wave is even bigger, but Anto and I get past it with ease. When the last wave in the set surges beneath me, I crest the peak and immediately see Anto sitting up on his board, a crazy grin plastered across his face.

Adrenaline gushes through me, along with relief. I'm shaking like a leaf.

"This is the fucking life, wha?" he screams.

I feel the wave of nausea rise up like a tide.

Lines publishes on August 1, 2021. Pre-order now from Amazon or sign up to get a notification email when it becomes available at www.dragonbrothersbooks.com/saltnewsletter

Books by James Russell
for younger readers

The Dragon Hunters, The Dragon Tamers and The Dragon Riders
are best-selling picture books for children aged 3-7,
and published in a dozen countries.

The five books in The Dragon Defenders series of junior novels
are for children aged 8-12. They are also best sellers, with over
50,000 copies sold.

Find out more at www.dragonbrothersbooks.com

Made in the USA
Las Vegas, NV
24 January 2024